TITANIAN FURY

"It's the Council. We've had a message from Caledonia. They're sending a delegation over to discuss trade. Janus has refused them. No one refuses Caledonia. We all know that. It's a death sentence. Astoria 5, gone. Paporia, gone. Luna 124, gone. We're next."

"Calm yourself," she said, for both their benefits. Caledonia had a reputation for devastation. "Your panic will not help the answers come. What is your question?"

"I don't know," he said, breathlessly. "The other Council Members, and everyone else at the Council really, are either desperately trying to contact Caledonia or racing to get to their transports and flee off planet."

"How long?"

"Days? Hours? I don't know."

Nothing she could do then, except sit tight and let everything shake out. Either she'd die, or she wouldn't. It was the wouldn't part that frightened her the most.

ALSO BY LINDA JORDAN

Falling Into Flight

Paradiso Stories

To the Stars & Back Again

Aboard the Universe

Love & the Aliens

The 12 Days of Christmas: An Off-Worlders Guide

Come on over to Linda's website and join the fun!

www.LindaJordan.net

Don't miss a release!

Sign up for Linda's Serendipitous Newsletter while you're there.

TITANIAN FURY

LINDA JORDAN

METAMORPHOSIS PRESS

For Michael & Zoe

CHAPTER 1 - CASSANDRA

MAMA ALWAYS TOLD STORIES TO PEOPLE. STORIES OF THEIR PAST AND the stories of their futures.

She used to say, "We have many possible futures, not just one. What is to come isn't set in stone, like I used to think. We can change the future."

Cassandra knew that now.

CASSANDRA LIVED in New Kasbah on Titania 37. A small backwater planet in an obscure system. The town had maybe three hundred beings living there, in a melange of cultures and species of all types. Most of them just trying to eke out a life. A great many of them were superstitious. The rest were on a spiritual journey. She catered to both.

Her shop stood just off the main marketplace on the ground floor of a native stone building. The yellowish brown rock was filled with miniature quartz crystals and resonated nicely with her energy. Most people believed rocks were dead. They lived and breathed just like everything else, except everything in their lifespans happened more slowly.

Her business was a magic shop, filled with rocks and crystals, wood and bone. She carried incense made from the dense osmiumwood of Copernicus 9. Also, Mithandalus sativus, a rare herb with a most piquant scent, almost like rosemary but more alien, with the power to attract what one most desires, whether a person acknowledged those wants or not. She carried handmade amulets, carved totems made from wood, bone and rock. Jewelry meant to protect and energize, not just look pretty. Candles made from beeswax that the candlemaker got from a local honey aviary. The candles were scented with the essences of amber, local figs, wine, peaches or cedar.

The candles were practical as well as magical. The winter windstorms often took out the village's power. Someday, the people in charge would figure out how to keep the connection from the solar panels and wind turbines intact. They weren't protected enough from the sand either. Piercing grains ripped the cables to pieces. They couldn't be buried because of the earth eaters, burrowing creatures that ate rock, sand and anything in their way. No one knew why, or if they did know, they weren't telling.

Even with wristbands and implants, humans, native Titanians, and even a few aliens, yearned to believe in magic. To believe the the multiverse had a plan for everyone. If only it could be found and understood.

Cassandra had the same yearning.

Unlike Mama, Cassandra had no stories of her own. Her only stories were those she told of others.

Her mother passed along the sight. Cassandra didn't ask for it and sometimes, didn't even want it.

Yet, unlike the Cassandra of old Earth, her prophecies were believed. They came true and people had noticed.

The air on Titania contained an element the humans commonly call divinity. It affected nearly all humans. It worked on the brain, opening it up to experiences those on old Earth searched for. Empathetic souls found themselves understanding others' feelings without having to be told. Some had a sense of connection to all living beings, including planets, and they become spiritual leaders. Still others like Cassandra, whose natural gifts ran towards divination, found themselves being able to foresee events much more regularly than they would have on old Earth. The air had changed humans in ways no one had expected.

At least that's what her mother told Cassandra. She'd been conceived onboard a ship and came to Titania still in the womb.

Cassandra was breathing divinity with her first breath. Maybe even before, since she had received all that her mother breathed.

Newcomers either adjusted to the changes in their systems or fled. Some of them in great psychological distress.

The morning that *it* happened was like any other. She rose and brewed her special tea, from a plant native to Titania. The natives called it something humans were unable pronounce, but the word had been translated as waking dream. It helped Cassandra flow from sleep into wakefulness.

The bitter dried herb steeped in water was palatable if a splash of goat's milk was added. Then she stirred in a spoonful of date sugar. The date palms were brought from old earth when Titania was first inhabited hundreds of years ago and planted in the moist valleys where they thrived and provided sweet fruit.

After tea, she dressed in a purple and black tunic made of a silky fabric, diaphanous black pants and sandals. She brushed her long dark hair and let it hang loose. People liked their fortune tellers to look a bit exotic.

Then she heated some flat bread that Sanya brought yesterday. Spread goat cheese on it, drizzled it with olive oil and savored the rich saltiness of it all.

Through the open window she could hear the bells on her door downstairs jangling.

She went to the window and looked down.

It was Colin, a member of the Council. Most times he came to see her when he was worried about his partner's health.

"What are you doing here so early?" she asked.

"Cassandra, I must talk to you. Now. Why don't you have a wristband?"

"They interfere with my energy. People who want to talk to me know where I live. Otherwise, they don't matter."

That was only partly true. She simply hated being hooked into the world by a piece of tech on her wrist. Or by anything. She preferred not to live in the everyday world, but to live in one of her own making instead. And people did know where she lived. She was easy to find.

It wasn't as if she couldn't afford a wristband. She could. And people had given her several. She simply hated them. Hated being monitored. Hated being part of the herd who the Council tracked.

Cassandra was an outlier and liked it that way. So far, the Council had let that slide for many of those who were unimportant in the great scheme of things. If they provided a service. Council Member Janus had been here just the other day, wanting to know why his daughter had run away from home.

"Let me in, please," said Colin.

"I'll be right down."

She poured another cup of tea, with milk and date sugar and then moved down the narrow stairway and through the darkened store, turning on small display lights as she went past.

She set her tea cup down and unlocked the door.

"Well?" she asked.

He moved past her into the store, sniffing in distaste.

"You've been burning fir incense again, haven't you?"

Fir incense was imported and extremely expensive. She really should ask Marita to cut back. Here in the desert it helped humans relax, so maybe it was worth it. For the natives, it provided more than a touch of the dramatic.

"That was Marita. She loves the stuff."

Marita came in every day and worked the store while Cassandra told people their stories, in the back room. Cassandra paid Marita what she could, as well as telling Marita her own story. Which Marita never tired of hearing. She was still waiting for some partner to fulfill her life.

Cassandra had given up on that long ago.

Colin went into the back room and sat down.

Obviously, this was going to take some time.

She followed him into the back, sipped her tea and set in on the table. Then snapped her fingers and the small glowies lit up the back room, dimly, for just the right ambience.

She dug out some matches and lit the candle and then a cluster of neronibush. Blew that out quickly, waved the cluster of oily leaves around the room and let the pungent smoke cleanse the space.

She silently called in her guides as Mama had taught her. The snow eagle who swooped down from tall peaks to catch its prey, seeing everything. The great hare who dug deep in the bowels of the planet, searching for sustenance. The tricolored gwandyuck, who loped across the deserts, carrying the wisdom of its forebears. And always the quick-thinking Kiria, who saw the unseen connections between everything.

She sat down on her plush chair and removed the ancient pack of cards from their green and purple embroidered cloth bag. She didn't use the crystal with Colin. He always needed something he could see.

Shuffling them, she asked, "What seems to be the problem?" She tried not to look ahead, but felt a terrible sense of foreboding. Something was really wrong.

"It's the Council. We've had a message from Caledonia. They're sending a delegation over to discuss trade. Janus has refused them. No one refuses Caledonia. We all know that. It's a death sentence. Astoria 5, gone. Paporia, gone. Luna 124, gone. We're next."

"Calm yourself," she said for both their benefits. Caledonia 96 had a reputation for devastation. "Your panic will not help the answers come. What is your question?"

"I don't know," he said, breathlessly. "The other Council Members, and everyone else at the Council really, are either desperately trying to contact Caledonia or racing to get to their transports and flee off planet."

"How long?"

"Days? Hours? I don't know."

Nothing she could do then, except sit tight and let everything shake out. Either she'd die, or she wouldn't. It was the wouldn't part that frightened her the most.

"Do you have a question yet?" she asked, looking into his dark eyes with the irises of spiraling golden brown, those eyes he used to mesmerize others.

"What should I do to help?" he asked, shrugging his narrow shoulders.

"That's a good start," she said, "now hold that question in your mind."

She shuffled three more times, had him cut the cards and then drew the top one. He turned it over, shivered and lay it on the table.

The card held a tall tower rising up through lightning-filled clouds, then shattering into pieces, reforming and shattering, again and again. People fell from the tower and the ground rose up, swallowing them.

"That can't be good," he said.

"There is no good or bad. Your life is what you make it. The cards are subject to interpretation. They are telling you to break things up. Break out of the pattern. What you've done before won't work any longer. Step out and let the old shatter. This is purification. What must be cleansed from your life? Whatever is left, will give you the tools to rebuild. Destruction must come before rebirth."

"So, I should just stand by and let the destruction happen? I can't do that. I took an oath. The Council exists to protect us all."

"Can you stop Caledonia?" she asked, in a more impassive tone than she felt.

"No. We can't match their military force."

"No one has ever come up with a good answer for that

question. What does a peaceful civilization do when faced with takeover by tyranny?"

"No, they haven't ever found an answer. But surely, we can't stand by and let Caledonia have this planet. Or obliterate it."

"Why would they want to keep it? There's no large money making industry. That's why our forebears chose it. There is enough, just enough, for all of us to live and share. Not enough riches for one of the big planet corps to bother with. We thought they'd leave us alone."

"Aye, we did," said Colin, leaning back in his chair, looking much older than his eighty-seven years. Wrinkles lined his forehead and the outer corners of his eyes. His skin the brown color of her tea, looked sallow somehow.

She drew another card.

Death.

Colin looked at it and groaned.

"All things must end. Let go and release. This is a transformation which will bring freedom. Know that death is coming and live each moment fully."

"So should I take Alexander and leave?"

"Are you asking me, or the cards?"

"You."

She sipped the bittersweet tea.

"I think you should do what you think is right. Would leaving here be any better? Where would you go? How would you live? Can Alexander make such a trip? Perhaps you should be asking him."

Colin put his head in his hands.

"He can't do it. He'd say he would try, but he couldn't really do it."

"Then your choice is clear," Cassandra said.

"To stay here and die?"

She sighed, "You know that the Death card is not necessarily about you dying. It is usually about the death of something. In this case, it could be the death of our republic. It could be the death of your latest artistic endeavor. Or the death of something you've been hanging onto that needs to be released like a bad habit."

"I know, I know," he said. "But usually I'm not asking about a tyrannical regime who uses extermination as a weapon."

She sat back, sipping the strong tea and trying to calm herself. The essence of neronibush smoke lingered in the room. She heard a key turn in the front door and the bells hanging on it tinkled like fairy music. Marita was here.

Should she tell her to go home? Take the day off?

If word got out the whole village would rip into chaos. People panicking, believing they could actually afford to get off planet.

But that was only for the ultra rich. Which most people weren't. Most of their ancestors had arrived on this planet with very few credits and those still remaining hadn't added a lot to that stash, some had even gone farther in the hole. Mostly, they made enough to get by. Food, water, housing, education and medical care were free. They were part of the payment for living on this planet and adding to the complexity of the community. Which helped everyone survive and even thrive.

But none of them were getting rich. Why would Caledonia want this planet?

She pulled another card. Ace of Worlds, Success.

The planets and suns on the face of it whirled around each other. Interrelated. Moving together, but in their own orbits, not hitting each other, but forming a whole system. Almost like a lock and key.

Titania 37 had something that completed Caledonia's plans. Something they needed to succeed, on their path to domination of this section of the multiverse.

"What?" asked Colin.

"I asked why Caledonia wanted the planet."

"Success? That makes no sense. What have we got that they want?"

"I don't know. We both need to think on that. But even if we knew, what difference would it make? If they wanted our date palms, could we stop them from taking them? If they want something that we're mining, could we prevent them from doing anything?"

"You're right. I should go home and take care of Alexander. Do what I can to keep people from panicking."

"Which will happen as soon as word gets out that council members are fleeing."

"Yes. Thank you," he said, standing. "I'll pay Marita. Blessings upon you Cassandra. I hope we meet again."

"So do I. Under better circumstances."

He nodded and left the room.

She gathered up the cards, shuffled them without thinking and slipped them into their cloth bag again.

Today would be a good day to stock up on food, make sure the water tanks were filled. Take care of business. And spread as much calm as she could around the village.

After Colin left, she told Marita what was happening. Her dark eyes went wide with terror, her dark skin paled.

"What are you going to do?" she asked.

"I'm going to make sure there's enough food in the house. And water. And supplies. And I'm going to tell people not to panic."

"Do you think they'll listen?"

"No, but I'm going to say it anyway. By my actions and my words. We will endure this. We need to come together and be strong."

"I'm coming with you. If that's all right. Closing the store, I mean."

"I don't think people will be coming in today. If they want me, they can find me, gathering food."

CHAPTER 2 - KALJU

Kalju Kepa paced around his tiny, gray quarters aboard the *Conqueror*. Gray, Caledonian ships were always gray.

To remind the Caledonians that nothing is black and white.

His mind raced as he went from screen to screen, looking up information about Titania 37. He must find the best way to seize control of the planet.

Rubbing his hands over his short-cropped coarse black hair, he exhaled deeply. This wasn't how he'd planned to serve his last few years. As Governor of a backwater planet. A bureaucrat.

The intended Governor, Aljius Palitan, had heart failure two days ago. There was no way he could continue.

Kalju had been … available. Removed from his most recent command, because of an issue with the Governor on Malion. They had disagreed on how to best quell the growing rebellion on that planet. It was Kalju's men who were being murdered and the Governor's plans left him powerless to protect them. He hadn't disobeyed orders exactly. He just hadn't obeyed them promptly.

Titania 37 was his punishment.

The ship would arrive in one day. He hated space travel. Tiny spaces with stuffy air, that never got clean enough and even though the oxygen was supposedly purified, it always smelled bad. Everyone got sick after space travel. It was expected.

Kalju sat on the bench. He felt weary of following meaningless orders. Someone else would have made a better governor here.

Yet, this seemed simple enough. Take control of the planet's small population. Commandeer the miners and extract the planet's reserves of scillion for the Caledonian military. It was a rare mineral, found only on certain planets and meteors. Highly unstable and explosive, but the engineers had found ways to deal with that, once the mineral was extracted.

The thought about simplicity niggled at him. Nothing that seemed simple ever was.

The problem was people. They were always the problem. They always had complaints, about a mineral they didn't even have any use for, being taken from them. And he wasn't skilled in dealing with people. He was a soldier, not a diplomat. However, that was the Caledonian way. Find a man's weakness and force him to either learn to overcome it, or fail completely.

He was going to overcome this weakness.

First, he needed to control the population centers.

There were three cities, more like small villages.

New Kasbah was the largest. About three hundred people, if you counted the natives who weren't humanoid. Half the population, mostly humans, lived at the Council Compound. The rest lived in the village. A quaint word, village. Then again, he supposed New Kasbah was quaint. A bit over a hundred people, not even a town. Most of the people just squatting on this planet at the edge of the civilized universe. Hoping to be left alone. Many of them probably criminals.

Santia, one of the other villages, centered around a gold mining operation. Maybe a hundred humans. And then Naritana, more gold mining. About seventy-five people, all human.

In other locations there lived small groups of two to six people. Farming or studying the planet. Titania wasn't suited for farming. These were people who grew whatever was possible to keep the other people on the planet alive. Why anyone would choose to live on such a sun-blasted piece of rock he couldn't understand.

The wall pinged in his cabin and a tiny door opened. In the slot sat a mug of what the ship called rania. It was no such thing. It tasted thin and bland. He picked up the steaming mug and drank it anyway. He needed clarity.

It he controlled those three population centers, he had the planet. Even though there were small populations of the natives, the Oachnik, scattered across the planet, they had never caused any problems for the humans. Mostly, they stuck to themselves. The Oachnik wouldn't be a problem, they were peaceful. Their weapons, if they had any, would be primitive. Not a threat to the Caledonians.

So he'd be based in New Kasbah. At the Council Compound. He'd send Lt. Generals Ritgan and Matton to the two mining operations. A three-pointed attack. Lock everything down and if the inhabitants were well behaved, give them a small amount of freedom.

Get in, extract the scillion and get out.

Perhaps it would be simple.

CHAPTER 3 - CASSANDRA

CASSANDRA TOOK TWO LARGE BASKETS WOVEN FROM DATE PALM leaves and handed one to Marita. They walked towards the center of the village, to the main market area. Vendors had their food laid out in the open fronts of their shops.

Most of them were open. Only a couple were closed. The fish seller, who often took days off to travel into the mountains and fish, was gone. The jeweler was closed as well. But she could have been delivering a piece, or haggling with the miners over stones they found. Or she could have fled off planet.

Cassandra chose to get her full allotment of goat and chicken meat, as did Marita.

"Cassandra, you never get your full allotment. Is there something you know that I don't?" asked the butcher, a tall, rangy woman.

Cassandra knew the butcher had heard the rumors and was pumping her for information.

"I think this is a good time to stock up and stay put," Cassandra said. "I feel changes coming, not all of them good. I will be like the sand in the desert. Indestructible. Sometimes stone, sometimes single grains."

"All right," the butcher said. "I've heard a lot of rumors flying. I'll follow your lead. You've never talked me into a wrong turn."

Cassandra nodded and moved on to one of the farmers.

The choice of fruits and vegetables was overwhelming. She chose melons and cucumbers, spicy greens, onions and garlic. Their baskets were nearly full.

She spoke to so many people, her head was spinning. They all had tales to tell about Council members and the wealthy families, who'd fled the planet. Seeking refuge on other worlds.

The air felt heavy with fear. She repeated her message about unity and digging in.

The last stop was the cheese shop. She chose hard and soft goat cheese. And two large containers of yogurt. They would last a while.

Then Marita and Cassandra carried all their food to her house, setting some things in her cooler. Freezing a few others. All of the homes in the village had back-up generators powered by the energy stored from each home's roof. It was an easy thing to switch from the New Kabash's massive power feed to one's home. Winter wind storms had given them much practice. Her house's storage wasn't quite enough to power both the store and the house. So, she normally switched off a lot of things. During a wind storm, it wasn't necessary to cool the store. No one would go out in a storm.

But it might be all she had in the near future. So she walked around the house, looking for all the things she could shut down.

If chaos became the rule of the day, she'd close the shop anyway. She could turn off the security system and drop the steel bars over windows and doors. The place had come with them. She had them withdrawn into the walls. They didn't exactly give the right vibe for her business.

So, she cleared off all the window sills and things from the doors, including the bells, and opened up the panels. Then pushed the switch and with a creak and a groan, the bars moved into place.

Marita took a deep breath behind her.

"It's like a prison."

"Yes, it is. But I might need it."

"I'm afraid," she said.

"Nothing wrong with that. Anyone who isn't doesn't have a brain in their head."

"Can I ask a favor?"

"What?"

"Can I stay with you? I could sleep in the shop. I haven't lived here long enough to qualify for more than a tiny apartment. It doesn't feel safe right now."

Cassandra thought for a minute. Marita lived on the far side of town. Where life was more expensive. Cassandra hadn't lived with anyone since Mama died. How would that be?

Still she quite liked Marita. The woman was young, smart and kind. Perhaps too kind. She'd been through hell, running from her crazy dysfunctional family, who lived in a religious cult and liked it. Once she'd come to Titania, she'd turned into an empath and still struggled with setting the boundaries with others.

It would be good to have another person around. Especially, if the world turned into what the cards had predicted.

"You can. I have an extra room upstairs. You won't want to stay down here, I might have to turn the cooling system off."

She pushed the button and the bars receded back into their pockets. Then put the string of bells back on the door. For now.

It took two of Titania's long days before Caledonians were on the ground. They declared martial law first and imposed a curfew. In those two long days of waiting Marita and Cassandra had been very busy.

Marita moved into Cassandra's house and they used all their credits to completely fill the food and water caches. They couldn't possibly eat it all, but at least it would be there to share with others.

The Caledonians stalked the streets with automatic weapons,

causing people to hide inside their homes. Only emergency services were open—health care and energy.

The Council was disbanded and a Caledonian Governor was given complete control. About a hundred beings worked and lived at the Council Complex. Cassandra wondered where they'd all gone. Perhaps most of them had gotten off planet.

From her neighbors, she heard only silence about the changes. No one was willing to even use their wristbands to communicate anything more than, "We're safe."

Marita could feel them through the walls. Safe, but alive.

Gradually, the messages came in through the wristbands. Marita heard it and repeated what was said.

"This is Governor Kalju Kepa. I am now in charge of this planet. You will follow my orders. With your cooperation, we can build a unique society. Tomorrow, I will lift the order of martial law. You may resume your businesses. There will be changes, of course. All weapons will be turned in to us. Expect us at your door so that this can happen peacefully."

Marita said, "He has a deep accent."

"Very few people have weapons. What does he expect to find?"

"It's true. People here are so poor."

Cassandra never thought of herself as poor, or the others around her. They weren't rich, but their lives were filled with all the good things in life. Healthy food, homes, medical care, peace. The community was small enough that unless you were a newcomer, everyone knew you.

What changes would the Caledonians bring?

That night soldiers rang the entryway signal. She went downstairs, switching on lights as she went. Marita followed her.

"We have come for your weapons," said the tall, pale man. He looked huge, full of muscle. He was sweating in the heavy black uniform.

It was warm outside, but the hot season of Titania's orbit was still to come.

"We don't have any weapons."

"Who else lives here."

"Just us," Cassandra said.

"Two women living alone, and you have no weapons?"

And there it was. The much talked about arrogance of Caledonia. Caledonian social structure was completely different from theirs. Titania didn't have a rigid patriarchy like they did, with all its ensuing problems. But she wasn't going to tell him that.

Mama had always said, "Don't try to change other people, it's a waste of time. It never works."

Cassandra said, "I've never needed weapons. This is a peaceful village."

He turned to his three companions.

"Search everywhere."

Two of them went up the stairs, the other began searching the shop, looking into storage cabinets and on shelves below the displays. Behind anything.

"We don't have any weapons," Cassandra said. "Please be careful. All of these things are fragile. Without my business, there will be no tax money for your government."

The soldier glared at her. She should have just shut up.

Marita moved forward and asked, "Excuse me. I'm a newcomer here and it took just days before the effects of divine in the air had an effect on me. Are any of you having any strange experiences?"

The man in charge looked at her like she had two heads.

There's a saying on Titania 37. "*You flow with the divine or it flows through you and tears you apart. It may or may not put you back together again.*"

Looked like he was going to be torn apart. He began walking around the shop, looking suspiciously at things.

"What is it you do here?"

Cassandra explained as best she could.

"So, you are a charlatan."

"I am no such thing. My mother was a seer and her mother before her. The divine in our air enhances my abilities."

"And yet you didn't see us coming."

"I saw you coming," she said.

"So you hid your weapons."

"I told you, I have no weapons. No one who lives here would attack me. I help everyone make choices for their future. I carry herbs and tinctures that they need. You are the only threat and I can guarantee you that there are no weapons on this entire planet that are a match for those you brought from Caledonia."

"What is this then?" he asked, picking up an athame.

"It is a ceremonial knife used in some rituals. A symbol. Go ahead, test it, it's not even sharp. Otherwise I wouldn't have imported it."

He tried to slash the gauzy fabric that pulled across the opening and only succeeded in snagging it.

"I still say you're a charlatan."

"Then you won't need to come here as a customer. You may change your mind once the divine works on you."

She'd seen it before. Newcomers from off planet. The most stubborn and unbelieving ones fell the hardest. It drove some of them crazy, because they couldn't admit to what was happening to them. The others tended to become fanatical about their gifts. It was a toss up which was worse.

The young soldier who'd been searching the shop looked at the man in charge and shrugged his shoulders.

"Go up stairs and help the others," the bully growled at him, then turned back to Cassandra and said, "So you think this divine is going to make us all go away?"

"I doubt that. But just as your coming here will change us, this planet will change you," she shrugged and sat on one of the metal chairs. It had been a long day and she felt exhausted. She didn't want to fight with this man.

Three pairs of footsteps thundered down the stairs.

"All we found were these," said one of the men, holding up her three kitchen knives.

The soldiers were all so young.

"What is this?" asked the bully.

"It's a knife for cutting bread and squashes. That one is for cutting meat and other vegetables. And that one is for slicing cheese and small vegetables. They are kitchen knives, not weapons," she said.

"You people may think you've beaten us, but you will find out we are invincible," said the bully. He flung the knives down on a display case, cracking the glass from the force.

"Very few in our village can afford weapons. We are not wealthy."

"You are lying. You've hidden your weapons. We will find them if we have to tear your village apart."

With that he spun on his heels and went out the door, waving to the others to follow.

Marita hurried to close the door and lock it.

Visions swam through her head, things she didn't want to see. The entire village torn apart by machines and burned. She could taste the smoke, smell the burnt out homes. Everyone who lived in the village herded into hastily assembled plastic buildings, which would disintegrate at the first fall windstorm.

"We need to leave. All of us," she said.

"Where will we go?"

"No idea. We need to talk to people. Tomorrow when they lift martial law, we'll have a sudden need to go to the market. Others may know somewhere we can hide."

"What should we do tonight?"

"Start packing," she said. "But only what you can carry. Choose wisely."

CHAPTER 4 - KALJU

KALJU STOOD IN THE NEAR-EMPTY COUNCIL CHAMBER. THE ROOM WAS shaped like an octagon with walls of a yellowish-brown stone and a large floor to ceiling window on each of the eight sides. Panels of windows stretched across the ceiling. All the walls and the ceiling contained inset panels which would roll out and close, shielding them from windstorms and perhaps even armed attack. Although they hadn't been used to repel the Caledonians. Most of the Council had already fled and there had been no resistance.

The view outside on the top of the butte was of green grass which went on for at least a mile. What a waste of water. The air in the room felt dry and arid, even with that lush foliage outside. Caledonian soldiers stood guard, two on each side of the building. The structure was high up, perched on top of the butte. The rest of the complex lay below ground. At the foot of the butte lay the landing pad and the town of New Kasbah. All under Caledonian control.

In the distance he could see the stony desert. Once this planet had abundant water. He knew enough geology to understand that the mountains and odd rock shapes had been formed by rivers. The planet was considered to be beautiful, if one liked deserts.

He'd had the former Council's servants strip all the wall hangings and curtains from the room. They moved all the furniture out except four straight chairs and a small, short table on which sat his tablet.

He might regret it. The sun was already blazing through the windows, overtaking the building's attempts to control the heat. He went to one of the windows and opened it, letting in the hot breeze. It felt fresher than the recycled air. He didn't trust the servants far enough to think they wouldn't try poisoning the air, water, or food.

He wiped the sweat that trickled down his brow and scrolled down, looking at the reports coming in.

Santia was under their control. So was Naritana. New Kasbah was locked down as well. Scillion would be mined at Santia and Naritiana.

In addition, two other Caledonian mining operations had landed in the areas where scans had shown scillion was plentiful, and were setting up. Troops were clearing out any humans or natives in those areas. Mining would begin tomorrow at all four sites.

He still had to deal with the three Council members and their families who hadn't fled Titania 37. And the townspeople of New Kasbah would keep his men occupied. Soldiers got stir crazy when they had nothing to do.

There was really no reason to keep any prisoners alive, but the Council had built such a sturdy prison beneath this great rock that he'd decided to make use of it.

Let Lt. General Farba learn what he could from them. The man was also overseeing the occupation of New Kasbah. That should keep him busy enough.

His Aide, Lt. General Matif, pushed through a door, carrying a tray.

A mug of hot rania sat on it.

"Governor," said the Lt. General.

"Thank you." Governor Kaju said, picking up the mug. He had

one of the Lieutenants and a couple of soldiers in the kitchen, overseeing food preparation to make sure everything was safe.

Trust no one on any captured planet. He'd learned that from his long career. He didn't trust the officers either. They were all working their way up. But his food and drink supply was as safe as he could make it, without overseeing every single detail personally.

He held his tablet over the mug and a chemical analysis of its ingredients came up. Safe to consume, it assured him. He sipped the hot liquid and savored the rich bitter flavor.

"Perfect," he said. "Not like that awful sludge on the ship."

"That wasn't rania," said Matif. "That was mud water."

"Ah, so you have discerning tastes?"

"Doesn't take much discernment to dislike the Fleet's rations, Sir."

Matif nodded. He would need to watch this one. This one definitely had his eye on moving up.

"What do you want out of life Lt. General?" he asked.

"The same as most. A good next meal, a beautiful woman, or two or three. Some leisure to enjoy life."

"A Governorship?"

"Maybe. If it was a proper planet. Not like this one. No insult intended."

"None taken. This is just a temporary post. We won't be here long, I hope."

"I'd like a planet with warm temps, but not too warm. Mild. An ocean with pristine beaches. Friendly natives or maybe none at all. And lots of raw materials to sell."

"Easy living?"

"Yes, easy living. But all those planets, or at least the ones we know of, have been taken or can't be."

"Well, they could be," said Kalju.

"But they'd cause a lot of fuss. We'd be attacked by the Consortium, or the Allies, or the Feds."

"True enough. It would be a struggle, but they *could* be taken."

They chatted a while longer. Yes, he'd need to keep an eye on Matif. An eye on all the Lt. Generals. They'd love to sabotage his mission here.

Every single one of them.

CHAPTER 5 - CASSANDRA

WHEN MARTIAL LAW WAS LIFTED THE NEXT DAY, THE MARKET WAS
flooded with buyers and sellers. And soldiers. They were spaced
every five feet, it seemed. Armed and ready for any problem.

The fruit sellers had marked up the prices for their over-ripe
bananas, apples and grapes. All had been grown aboard some
supply ship and sold to planets they passed. None of the fruit ripe
when picked, she'd heard. Now the smell of it bananas was
overwhelming. They weren't brown on the outside, but their
inside was mushy.

There were a couple of live goats outside the butcher shop,
someone looking to sell them to the butcher for meat. No one
knew what the future would hold for New Kasbah and there was a
thick tension in the air. The soldiers' presence just added to that.

Most of the villagers had run out of food, they hadn't stocked
up like Cassandra. The Oachnik had of course. They were native to
this planet and though they were naturally nomadic, she had
never seen them unprepared for any emergency. They understood
the harshness of the desert in a way humans didn't.

Cassandra approached Xixia, the head of the clan who she
knew most closely. She had helped her through a difficult time
when one of her daughters died several years back.

"Xixia, how are you this fine morning?"

"We live on, though the weight of the air makes us feel old and humble. And how does Cassandra on this brilliant day?"

"I also live on, although life is being threatened."

They examined potatoes covered with brown rotten spots as they talked, so as not to draw the attention of the soldiers.

"How threatened is life?" Xixia asked, her tongue clicking as she rubbed one large cupped ear with a furred, long-fingered front paw.

The Oachnik were taller than most humans, with gaunt, furry bodies and long wooly tails. Their ears were large and sat on the top of their heads. Oachnik faces looked almost mouselike with whiskers. Their back legs long and powerful, knees bent backwards. They were fabulous at leaping. Hands were thick and padded and Oachnik could as easily run on four legs as two, although their fingers were thin and dextrous enough to do fine weaving.

"I do not like these soldiers. They do not mean any of us well. We are not important to their plans on this planet."

"You have seen this?" she asked.

"I have."

"Hm," she said, clicking and holding up a peach that was unripe. "Yesterday, we were just thinking that being settled has made us lazy. And soft."

"It is so."

"It is time for us to move on." This time Xixia used the plural us, as in all her tribe.

"Are you able to take us with you?"

"Who us?"

"All of the village. We humans are very soft and we have nowhere else to go. But we must get out before the soldiers take us all away."

Xixia was silent. Thinking. Perhaps speaking silently to the other clan heads. Oachnik could do that.

Finally she said, "The other clans will not wait for you. We will take you. Tonight. When the sand moon rises meet us behind the group of rocks just past the village."

Xixia cocked her head indicating where she would meet them.

Xixia continued, "Be silent and bring only what can be carried. Bring food and water. We will find no water for two nights of walking. We do not know how Cassandra can get her clan ready so quickly, but it is as you say. They do not mean any of us well. We have seen it in their eyes, heard it on their breath. They are unnatural."

"Tonight then," Cassandra said, softly.

Xixia nodded and traded a small bag of dates for several peaches that were turning brown. They smelled delicious.

Cassandra took a deep breath. There was much to do. She had to contact as many villagers as possible. Without the soldiers overhearing.

She had Allen, the fruit and vegetable seller, scan the wristband and bought two overripe peaches. Then she returned the wristband to her pocket. She would have to remember to leave it behind tonight so no one could track her.

Cassandra bit into the soft peach, tasting the juiciness of it. It was the flavor of summer. A richness, meant to be savored.

Marita came up to her and Cassandra gave her the other peach. Then filled her in on the conversation she had with Xixia.

"Tell those that you can. Have them discretely spread the word. No wristbands, otherwise they'll be able to track us. Bring food and water that they can carry and get out of the village while it's dark and the soldiers can't see them," said Cassandra.

She worried about how they could all escape the village, in such a short time. Silently. Without the soldiers finding out.

At least they didn't have to worry about those who lived in the consulate and hadn't had time to flee. It was surely locked down already. She'd probably never see Colin again. She hoped he and Alexander were safe.

The villagers had lived in this desert for a long time. Some of them their entire lives. They understood what going into the desert meant. It was a place where one's actions meant the difference between living and dying.

Still, they were as Xixia had said, soft.

Cassandra continued to shop, leisurely, buying things she didn't need. Talking discreetly to everyone and making sure they knew what to do if they wanted to leave. Some would not be coming. Those too elderly or physically unable to trek through the desert. Word would get passed along discreetly.

"I'll take over Jake's tonight and those of us staying will have a helluva party," said Angel, the meat vendor. "A distraction."

He'd been injured decades ago in an accident. He walked with the support of metal canes, having never been able to afford new legs.

Cassandra nodded and reached out to touch his arm.

"May the sun shine down his blessings on you."

"Always does," he grinned.

"Tell those that stay, I'll leave my refrigeration on. And an extra key above my sign. There will be some food in my refrigeration unit. And extra water. Take what you need and lock up when you leave. Food may become scarce."

"I'll do that and thankee."

By the end of the day, her feet ached. Cassandra and Marita moved slowly back to her house, weighed down with cloth bags filled with fabric, beads, more food and water.

"I should have spent the afternoon resting."

"Well, go slow now," said Marita. "I'll pack the food. You've got two hours to pack and close up the house."

She'd sampled so much food at the market, there was no need for to eat a meal. Cassandra pulled the bars down over the windows and doors, locking them. Then put an extra key on the ledge above her sign outside. Turned off all non-essential systems, setting the backup power systems to turn on automatically.

Then she slipped out of her shoes and put on heavy cotton pants and a long-sleeved shirt. Socks and light boots. She packed an extra set of clothes and a jacket. Setting aside a heavy hooded shirt for tonight. All of the clothes were a pale reddish brown. The color of the landscape.

She set the wristband on the table near her bed. Free of one thing at least.

Cassandra sat crosslegged on her bed and and asked the multiverse for clarity. What did she really need to bring along?

In the end, she packed her favorite deck of tarot cards. An artist, Jakka Goudin, had hand painted them with Cassandra's requests for each of the cards' symbols. They were illuminated with gold leaf. She slipped them into their embroidered bag, made by one of the villagers, Sara. Then tucked in a quartz crystal and put them into the pack.

She had two changes of clothes, a light jacket and a scarf for her head and face. Still the pack felt heavy with food and water. Nothing to be done about it. She put an amber pendant around her neck and then turned out the lights.

Marita followed her out the door. Cassandra locked it and slid the key into her pack.

They made it down two streets before spotting any soldiers. The doorways were cluttered with pots of flowers and even trees. None of the village had been built at the same time, so there were pillars and porches that stuck out here and there, even though the buildings were close together, there were spaces between them. Places to hide. She hoped soldiers weren't hiding in any of them.

They made their way little by little to the edge of town. Cassandra's heart was in her throat the entire time. Pounding with fear.

At the edge of the village soldiers patrolled. She watched, crouched in the shadows of the rising sand moon, called that by the Oachnik. The humans called it Cobweb moon, because of its spiderweb appearance and in reference to some old play the planet was named after.

Behind the rock formation lay the meeting spot. It was only six meters away. But there were five soldiers with big guns.

Several explosions sounded behind Cassandra and Marita. In

the center of town. It sounded like someone had stolen some explosives from the mines and was shooting them off for fun. It happened now and again.

The explosions were followed by drunken yelling. She recognized Angel's voice. He was doing his part to cause a distraction.

The guards consulted and three of them ran off towards the commotion.

Then out from behind the rock came Xixia. She wobbled along, using a gnarled stick as a cane. One soldier yelled at her and she slowly moved towards them, with a befuddled look on her face.

One of the soldiers began to manhandle her and Xixia flipped her cane up and clipped him on the head. He dropped to the sand, out cold. She did the same to the other one before he could get his gun up.

Then she motioned and streams of people came flooding out of the shadows of the five streets that ended on that side of town. The villagers ran to the safety of the rocks.

"It is time," said Xixia. "Are all your people here?"

Cassandra looked around. There were about two hundred who lived in the village. Probably half of those were Oachnik. About twenty-five humans were staying behind. Were there seventy-five humans here? She couldn't tell.

But they needed to leave. The soldiers would return as soon as they found out they weren't needed. And they'd find the two men down, who would probably be conscious by then, if they weren't already.

Cassandra nodded and said quietly, "If any of you have wristbands, take them off and toss them out on the other side of the rock. We don't want them to be able to track us."

Everyone nodded, but didn't move.

"Now. We're leaving now. No talking, no noise."

Only two people tossed their wristbands. She hoped that meant the others had already left theirs behind. Cassandra turned to Xixia and nodded.

They moved through a cut in between the next rock formation. The light was dim still and it was slow going.

The wind picked up and sand began to blow. Cassandra moved her scarf up over her mouth and nose. At least the wind would cover some of their tracks in the sand.

They walked over the sharp rocks as silently as possible.

Every now and then they started a night snake and it slithered away. The Oachnik halted then and waited. Night snakes were white and considered sacred. It was bad luck to bother them.

When they reached a large overhang, one of the Oachnik, a young male, whose name Cassandra didn't know, motioned them to crowd in underneath. Three Oachnik consulted and they split the humans up into three groups.

Xixia said, "We must go in smaller groups. We will travel in different directions. It will make us more difficult to find. We will meet up later."

"How much later?" asked Naylon, one of the produce sellers. He pulled back his smooth, long, dark hair into a thong. His light tea colored skin blended in with the tan robes he wore over long pants and shirt.

Just looking at his clothes made Cassandra feel overly warm. She wore only a thin shirt and pants and felt hot from the exertion.

"It takes us six nights to travel to the caves. With you we will go slower. And we will be hiding more often. Who can say?" asked Xixia.

People divided themselves into three groups and the three younger Oachnik led them all in different directions. Cassandra and Marita were in a group with Xixia.

"Why do the young ones lead?" asked Cassandra.

"They spend more time traveling. They know the most current ways in which the desert has shaped herself. It gives them experience leading. They are only our traveling leaders for now. Later, when they are older, those most gifted with leading might become clan heads. Do not worry, your people are as safe with one as with another. It is the desert who will make the decision."

"Or the Caledonians."

"They follow, but we will lose them soon. Now that we are in smaller groups, we will move faster and use paths the strangers will never find."

Their group was the last to leave, there were about fifty of them, split between human and Oachnik. The first group had gone left, the second right. Their group moved straight ahead. They wove through the twists and turns of tall, thin rock canyons. At several points the trail was so narrow Cassandra could touch the smooth rock on both sides of her.

At the tail end, one Oachnik brushed the thin layer of sand that lay over the rocks with sticks and a broom-like tool, obliterating the line of footprints.

At one point the Oachnik heard a flyer coming and everyone hid under an overhang. They weren't necessarily searching for them. Would the Caledonians even care if humans went missing? They just didn't want to jeopardize the reason they came to the planet. It could have been a mining flight, or something else. Cassandra wasn't sticking her head out to see what kind of ship it was, even if she'd be able to tell in the near dark.

CHAPTER 6 - KALJU

Kalju stood in the center of New Kasbah. The empty village square.

Fury clenched his fists, but he managed to keep a look of questioning frozen on his face. Unwilling to let his emotions show.

Lt. General Farba stood in front of him. Panic written across his wide features, the man's gray eyes glanced wildly about. Farba's black uniform looked neat enough, but his shoulders slumped, as if indicating the sloppiness of his command.

Kalju smiled inwardly. Farba may think he was on his way up, but Kalju would see that didn't happen. Lt. General Matif had been right, Farba had let most of the villagers slip away overnight.

They waited for Farba's men to bring any sign of the villagers.

Kalju counted the seconds and minutes. Seemingly patient, his mind reeled with paranoia.

Had Farba done it on purpose?

The villagers might be sabotaging the mining operations right now. If the mining mission failed, then he, Kalju, would have failed.

No, Farba was incompetent. The son of a cabinet member who'd been promoted above his competence.

Finally Kalju heard rustling and from down one of the side

streets moved a squad of soldiers, hustling villagers in front of them. Villagers who clearly had just woken up. A shirtless man, limping and trying to help an old woman hobbling along with a cane. Every single one of them was old or had problems walking. A great bear of a man using mechanical legs. A middle-aged man so skeletal as so be recovering from a harsh illness vomited as soon as they stopped. There were only a dozen of them.

"Found them in the pub, sir."

Somehow, overnight the entire village had emptied. A couple hundred people, gone. Vanished into thin air.

Lt. General Farba found his balls somewhere and began interrogating the villagers.

"Where is everyone else?" he yelled at the old woman with the cane.

"Don't you take that tone with me, young man. How should I know? I'm not in charge of them," she said, a note of anger in her voice.

Farba slapped her and she fell sideways onto the large burly man with the mechanical legs. He caught her, and helped her upright again. Restrained her from taking the walking stick to Farba.

Kalju said nothing.

Minutes later, the remaining six squads returned. With no one else.

"Secure these prisoners," said Kalju to the soldiers. Then to Farba, "Meet me up top in an hour."

Lt. General Farba nodded, his lips tight and grim.

Kalju turned and walked back towards the butte followed by his security detail, a five minute walk. As he passed through the barren sandy area populated only by rocks, he didn't touch the sweat trickling down his temples. Damned hot planet. He'd be pleased to get this assignment over and done.

He recorded his complaints against Lt. General Farba and put them on record. Adding in his concerns about the colonists damaging the mining operation. He sent copies of the report to Lt.

Generals Ritgan, Matton and the others, telling them to add extra security.

As he entered the butte through the Council doors, the cool breeze made him feel suddenly chilled.

What if Farba was in it with all the others? What if they meant to bring him down? He needed to keep a closer eye on them. He should visit the operations. Without warning. Otherwise that would give them time to hide any problems they were having.

He strode through the highly lit lobby. The floors of polished stone. The room didn't look like it was cut out of the solid rock of the butte.

Walls with transparent waterfalls, the sound of which muted any echoes. The spray of water filled the air, making it feel otherworldly. Green vines grew everywhere. Red, white and yellow tropical flowers adorned some of the plants. The interior of the butte looked like a jungle world. It must have cost a fortune.

In complete contrast to the village. which looked ramshackle compared to this luxury. The Council obviously had money and lots of it. Kalju had been unable to find any record of it. He presumed that one or several of the Council Members who fled had taken it with them.

Farba had been useless in gaining any information from the three remaining Council Members, having beaten two of them to a bloody pulp and threatened to kill the woman's daughter. Why would anyone make a woman a Council Member? Women were too dangerous to be trusted.

He took the elevator up to the top floor where the Council chamber sat. His security took their places out in the entryway around the elevator.

The guards were still outside the chamber, arrayed across the top of the butte. The only attack here would come from the air. The cliff sides were too high and steep for most humans to scale. Could the Oachnik climb?

He'd have to look into that. Maybe he should post more guards at the bottom of the butte, around all sides.

An hour later Farba knocked on the inner door of the chamber.

"Enter," said Kalju

"Governor," said Farba, entering.

He stood at attention until Kalju looked up from the table and his tablet.

"What are you going to do about the missing villagers?"

Lt. General Farba's eyebrows raised and his mouth opened.

He clearly hadn't expected the question, or the chance to redeem himself. Idiot.

"I don't know, Sir."

"Do you want Caledonia's mission on this planet to fail?"

"No sir."

"Well, then what? You have to assume that they have escaped and will do everything in their power to hinder us."

"I should hunt them down, Sir."

"Then what?"

"Kill them?"

He really was a spineless worm. If Kalju had the power to remove him from the mission, he would. His superior, Commander Zakra could. He'd include Farba's failings in the next report.

"Or imprison them. Are the prisoner barracks complete?"

"Yes, Sir."

"Well then kill one of them, to make a statement. Imprison the others. Maybe you can get some information out of them. I doubt it, considering the progress you've made on the Council Members. Dismissed."

"Thank you, Sir," said Farba, turning and almost running from the room.

How could such a complete worm of a man be the one to beat a prisoner senseless?

Kalju made a note in his report about Lt. General Farba's lack of a plan to deal with the escaped prisoners. Then he set up an ample security detail for the perimeter of the base of the butte.

CHAPTER 7 - CASSANDRA

THE NIGHT SEEMED ENDLESS. HER MUSCLES, NOT USED TO WALKING SO much, felt rubbery. They had stopped to rest several times, but it wasn't enough.

The moon gradually rose higher and sometimes the rocks were low enough that some light shone on the ground. Mostly not. It was slow going and only by following the person in front of her could she find her way.

The sand moon set and they'd climbed high enough on the rocks to see the horizon. The sunrise was glorious in crimson and salmon colors. Then she saw Xixia place her hand on the rock and a hole opened up, just like a door swinging open. Stone grated upon stone, making a deep grinding sound. Cool air escaped from the depths of the planet. It smelled moist and had a freshness about it that Cassandra had never experienced before.

They followed her inside to complete darkness.

Off to the left felt open and empty. Cassandra clung to the solid rock wall on her right.

As they slowly shuffled forward, hands feeling the way down a wall, someone in front turned on a small battery powered light. It illuminated a steep, narrow pathway. The rest of the cavern floor lay far below. It was immense. Smooth, flat boulders lay as if sprinkled here and there by a giant. She couldn't tell from this far away if they had been put there by water or a volcano. Either was possible. Or perhaps they'd fallen from the ceiling.

Behind her, a young Oachnik stood by the entrance, moving hands over the stone. The opening closed with the same grating grumbling sound that echoed across the cavern, amplifying it. No one would be following them silently at least.

Cassandra was about halfway back through the group and it took a long time to make the steep climb down. There were more than a few children, parents carrying younger children and older people, all of whom were exhausted. She helped Magda, who walked in front of her. Carrying the older woman's bundle of belongings and Gene, who was in front of Magda took the woman's arm and supported her weight. The walkway was barely wide enough for two people to walk side by side.

The Oachnik carrying the light had reached the cavern floor and stood resting, illuminating the pathway for those still coming down.

It seemed to take forever, but she finally make it down to more solid ground and put Magda's bundle down near where Magda had collapsed. Magda looked up at her gratefully and Cassandra smiled at her.

She walked farther out into the cavern and plunked down near the others already there. Sitting on a higher flat area, she crossed her legs and took off the pack. Her legs ached from the long march and she massaged them as she stretched. Even her fingers felt weary.

What time was it? Surely it was morning up above on the surface.

The Oachnik who had been leading us, consulted with three other younger ones.

"We will rest here for many hours, eat and sleep," the tallest one said.

Cassandra pulled some roasted goat meat, cheese and flatbread from her pack. The meat wouldn't last very long, even in the cooling container. Maybe another day. She rolled them up in the flatbread and ate, savoring the smoky flavor of the meat.

She didn't want to eat, just to sleep. But her body needed the food.

She could see Gene pushing Magda to eat before she slept. She was arguing with him. He continued to push at her and eventually she gave in and ate. Probably so he'd leave her alone and let her sleep. Although she was smiling as she chewed. As if enjoying the attention.

Was a fire brewing between the two of them? Interesting. Cassandra hadn't noticed that before. This exodus was shaking everything up.

She finished the food, swallowed a mouthful of water and pulled her sleepbag out of the pack, set the temp to 15.5.C and curled up inside it.

When she woke, the cavern was dimly lit. Sounds of snoring and deep breathing echoed across the massive cavern. Cassandra sat up, pulling the sleepbag close around her neck. The air felt cold. Three Oachnik sat at the base of the pathway up to the door. They were huddled together, speaking with that vacant look Oachnik got when they communicated telepathically. Present, but their concentration elsewhere.

All the other humans and Oachnik were sleeping. She lay back down and slept longer.

The next thing she knew, nearly everyone was up, rustling around. Putting belongings away, getting out food. Waking up.

Cassandra felt groggy and out of sorts. Like she was a book that had been shelved upside down. Of course few on the planet had seen books. She sold a few books, ones printed up and bound at the consulate. They were a luxury item, but for studying things like tarot spreads, invaluable. Most people had books read to them, while they did other things.

She forced herself out of the sleepbag and rolled it up, stuffing the small bundle into her pack. She ate more goat meat, cheese and one of the peaches from the market yesterday. The juice from it tasted intense and almost rich.

Marita came over and sat nearby. She sipped on her water bottle.

"I've never camped before. It was interesting sleeping on rocks."

"Mmm." Cassandra mumbled through her mouthful of goat meat. She wasn't a morning person.

"Where do you think they'll take us?"

"No idea. Why don't you ask them?"

"Should I?"

Cassandra nodded, smiling more brightly than she felt.

Marita nearly leapt up and walked over to the three youngsters who appeared to be leading them. Oh, to be young again. Not for the entire world.

It didn't take long for everyone to roust themselves and get moving again. When they left the big cavern, Xixia, who was behind Cassandra let out a deep breath. Cassandra turned to her and looked.

"I am relieved to be moving along. That cavern is not a safe place."

"Why?"

"Too large and exposed." She paused, took another deep breath and said, "Solshun doesn't know, but it was the place where many of our ancestors were massacred."

"By who?"

"The Gonsha."

"I thought the Gonsha were a myth," Cassandra said.

Xixia's eyes widened and she slowly shook her head. "Not a myth. Two generations ago, we killed all of them."

Cassandra had been told about the Gonsha. They were two and half meter tall humanoids with thick scraggly bluish white fur, a thin tail nearly as long as they were tall used for balancing and fighting. Gonsha had sharp claws on their six fingers and toes and three rows of sharp teeth. The stuff of nightmares, they could see in the dark and made curved swords and knives from alloys of various metals found deep beneath the surface.

They were known as fierce warriors who had spent a good deal of energy defending their territory. The Oachnik did the same, although they weren't as skilled at metal making or killing.

"How did you kill them all? And how do you know you got all of them?"

"We haven't seen them around. I don't really know how it was accomplished, but I do know we invoked the assistance of Kaiuun."

Kaiuun was one of the Oachnik deities. A creator/destroyer goddess who could be likened to Kali from old Earth. That was heavy magic indeed.

"Will you do the same to chase away the Caledonians?" she asked.

"I cannot make such a decision and no one besides you has suggested such a thing," she said, giving her a wary look.

Cassandra felt like she'd made a misstep.

"I'm sorry, I shouldn't say the first thing that pops into my head."

"When we destroyed the Gonsha, there were consequences. Our people lost a priceless gift."

Xixia just looked down at her own hands. Cassandra waited for her to continue, following the appropriate Oachnik timing for such a revelation.

Xixia continued, "Our people used to be able to command the wind, the water and the other elements. Our ancestors sacrificed that gift for Kaiuun's help. I am not sure the price was worth it. We have been lost souls ever since that time."

Cassandra nodded, but didn't understand. The Oachnik had always seemed to her to be completely connected to the planet. At home with it in a way humans weren't.

They continued to move through narrow tunnels that plunged deep beneath the surface. Would she ever see sunlight again?

Most of them walked through darkness for hour after hour.

There were lights at the front, middle and the back of the line. But in such narrow spaces mostly it was dim light to almost complete darkness. It was slow going.

How many days would it take to get to where the Oachnik were going? Were the other two groups moving through similar terrain?

Once as they passed through a small cavern, the entire ground shook and a few small rocks fell from above.

Xixia clucked with her tongue.

"They are using explosives."

"The Caledonians?"

"Yes."

"Are they trying to flush us out?"

"Who knows? There have been rumors they are mining in places where they should not."

Cassandra asked, "What do you mean *places where they should not?*"

"There are places where the caves are fragile, or that are sacred to our gods. It is forbidden to go to those places. The Caledonians are newcomers and may not know about those places. Why else would they do such things?"

"I expect they wouldn't respect your customs, even if they knew them. They only respect their own."

Xixia moved her hands across her face, all fingers crossed in such a way as to gesture, *Goddess help them, then.*

What did she think her goddess would do? Which goddess was she invoking? The Oachnik had a complicated pantheon of deities that Cassandra had barely unraveled in her many decades of life. Which didn't mean she discounted the power of their deities. She'd seen enough things to have great respect for their beliefs, whether it was called the laws of science or Kaiuun in action, they understood their planet on a level that humans didn't.

CHAPTER 8 - KALJU

KALJU WALKED OUTSIDE THE COUNCIL CHAMBER ON THE TOP OF THE grassy butte. The wind almost blew him over. A nearby guard saluted him and he nodded. Kalju walked across the butte, hot wind streaming through his cropped hair. It carried fine grit and the scent of dirt with it.

There wasn't enough work for him to do here. He disliked having to keep such close watch on all his Lt. Generals. Annoyed that he hadn't been able to bring along men he chose. Trusted men.

Farba had not been able to find the villagers yet. It was as if they melted into the stones in the nearby desert. The planet was riddled with underground caverns, which might be why they'd found scillion there.

Lt. General Ritgan was having equipment problems, as all the operations seemed to be. The mining equipment brought from Caledonia wasn't working properly and they'd had to make modifications. Which was slowing things down. They expected to be up and running in the next couple of days.

Which meant he'd definitely need to do surprise inspections and have a communications blackout between the operations. If such a thing was even possible these days. Soldiers from one division generally knew someone from another division. They kept in touch with wristbands. Too much communication was not a good thing, but the damn wristbands had come in handy more than once, so he'd decided to let the men keep them.

And it was the Lt. Generals, not the troops he worried about. They were the ones most likely to be colluding. He wished once again for men he could trust. Even men planted in each of the divisions as spies would have helped, but there hadn't been time.

This entire occupation had been rushed for some reason. As if the presence of scillion on the planet had just been discovered. Or the government was planning a large scale military build-up of weapons.

If that was the case, he wanted to be part of the fighting. Not sitting here on some backwater planet supervising a mining expedition.

At sixty-three, he was in the prime of his career. Not physically, but mentally. He was sharp and needed to be using his intellectual and planning skills. His superior, Commander Zakra, must know what was going on. Was he setting Kalju up for failure? Keeping him secluded out here?

Were they *all* out to get him?

He rubbed the grit from his eyes. He hated this planet.

From the minute they'd landed, he'd begun to feel unstable. He'd heard rumors about the divine and scoffed at it. As had every Caledonian he knew. It was just a folk tale. They'd analyzed the air and there was nothing in it, but sand. Then again, sensors didn't register everything, just the most common elements. They hadn't caught the poison gas on Natalbia, which had killed hundreds of soldiers before they got masked up.

He sent a message asking the scientists at each of the mining sites to do a deeper scan of the air. To search for unknown elements.

He turned and went back inside, closing the large glass door and sealing it behind him. Then took the elevator down, his security detail went with him.

On the fifth floor from the bottom, he got out. This was where the prisoners were being held. The hallway was completely white. Sterile. Easy to spot anyone who shouldn't be there. The cells all had open fronts with bars, there was no privacy here. There were so many cells in the butte that every person had a separate one.

Nearly all the villagers were huddled into one back corner or the other, on their bunk. Silent. Although the big man with mechanical legs stood at the front, hands gripping the bars. He looked almost menacing.

"Why are we being held prisoner?" the man asked. "We've done nothing wrong."

Kalju ignored him and walked on, nodded to guards as he passed them and they saluted.

At the end of the hallway were the three council prisoners. None of the cells facing each other and each one separated by an empty cell in between. First was the woman. She was huddled on her bunk and stared at him warily.

Then the old man. He was allowed to have his woman in the same cell with him, although Kalju assumed they'd learned that was a curse more than a blessing. They sat on the bunk, silent and looked up at him as he walked past.

In the last cell was a middle-aged man. His face and body badly bruised.

Kalju nodded at the guard to unlock the cell and let him in. The guard did, bringing in a chair that sat in the hallway for him to sit on.

"You can stay out here," Kalju said, to his detail. "This man is not a threat to me."

They looked concerned, but did as he asked.

Kalju sat in the chair. The man cowered on the bunk, not meeting his eyes.

"I apologize for what Lt. General Farba did to you," Kalju said. "He has only one way of working, it seems."

The man looked at him, as if reassessing the situation.

Kalju continued, "Have your injuries been seen to?"

"Yes," said the man.

"You are Colin Schuante, Council Member, am I right?"

"Yes."

"I need information from you."

"I told the other officer everything I know, which isn't much."

"Was the Council selling scillion?"

"What? No. Scillion is a banned mineral. We are not large enough, or powerful enough to attempt such a thing."

"Someone on the planet was and I need to know who the buyer was."

"I have no idea. Titania 37 has very few exports. A small amount of gold to whoever will buy it. We sell some dates and goat cheese to supply ships, but that's it. If someone was selling scillion they were doing it without the Council's knowledge or permission."

"If you had to guess, who would you say was selling it?"

"Someone would need to have the mining equipment. They'd need to have a way to get it off planet without anyone noticing, so it couldn't come through our port here. And they couldn't be selling much or the ship traffic would get noticed," said Colin.

"And?"

"I don't know. That's all I can think of. If it was one of the miners, they'd all have to be involved, otherwise someone would notice. It's possible that someone was living in a remote area and mining it and exporting it. We would have no way of tracking them. This is a small planet and we don't have full coverage of communications or surveillance."

"Would any of the other Council Members know or be involved?"

"I very much doubt it. None of us needed money that badly. Our families bought in to the Councilship when the planet was colonized. We all hold a stake in the mining corporation and profits are good."

"Sometimes, people are greedy," said Kalju.

"Yes, I suppose that's possible," said the man, running a hand through his greasy, disheveled hair. "Most of them fled, though. Don't know if they'll ever try to come back."

"And none of them were having financial problems?"

"They wouldn't have admitted it to me, if they did. That would have been a sign of weakness."

"How many fled?" asked Kalju, even though he knew the answers.

"There were fifteen Council Members. I have no idea how many are still on the planet or how many fled."

"Can you give their names?"

"I already told the officer all this."

"Did you now?"

Farba hadn't relayed the information. Another black mark against him.

"Yes. Before he beat me. I will tell you if you'd like."

"No, I'll get it from him. Tell me, what do you know about the divine?"

The man stared at him, then began to speak. "The divine is a microscopic life form as best our scientists can tell. They couldn't find any records of anything like it on any other planet. It works on humans' brain functioning, and on Oachnik too, apparently. Changes the way we sense things and sometimes the way we think. When this planet was first colonized by humans, it mutated quickly. As far as we can tell, if a person accepts the changes that the divine brings, it's easy to live with."

"What if one doesn't accept this invasion?"

"The human is driven to insanity, and often death by suicide. Some have remained sane by leaving the planet quickly."

"So, either surrender or leave?" asked Kalju, fists clenched behind him.

"That's what we've found. There may be other ways, but here on Titania 37 we've always been short on scientists. Money is tight and scientific research can command a high price. Our initial research was done solely by those specializing in the soil sciences.

We could only afford to hire scientists who would bring us a financial benefit."

"Your discussion of this life form, even the naming of it, seems too religious."

"It does, doesn't it. Blame our ancestors for that. Are you going to kill us?"

Kalju looked at him, keeping his face and body absent of any telling gestures by long habit. Stoneface, they called him behind his back.

"I don't know. I don't know what the future will bring. Our plan was to come in, mine the scillion and leave. If all goes as planned and all the planet's inhabitants leave us to work without interference, we'll be pleased to see the last of this planet and leave it to you. That's all I have to offer at the moment."

"That's enough. Thank you," said the man.

Kalju rose from the chair, ignoring the pain in his knees. He was not getting too old for this work. He just needed to have them seen to. When he got back to Caledonia.

CHAPTER 9 - CASSANDRA

AT ONE POINT, SOLSHUN LED THEM INTO A MEDIUM-SIZED CAVERN. Everyone squeezed in, sitting down to rest and eat a quick meal.

Cassandra's goat meat was gone, so she ate hard cheese and a few dates. She hoped wherever the Oachnik were taking them had plenty of food.

They ate a similar diet to humans. Proteins balanced with vegetables, fruits, a few grains and some dairy. They herded the small, red furred, hooved etalia for their milk and kept them as pets, sacrificing the elderly and infirm, for their meat. The fallen horns were used to carve drinking vessels and beads, and the hides used as blankets.

Cassandra sat next to Marita, who was uncharacteristically quiet. Which suited Cassandra. She was used to living alone and greatly valued her solitude. This trek into the desert was far too social.

She chewed the partially dried dates, savoring their sweetness. After finishing, she lay back on her pack and had just drifted off for a nap when Solshun said, "It is time to move on."

Cassandra glanced up at a flashing movement near the ceiling of the cavern. There, among the rocks on the side, she caught a glimpse of three Gonsha with long white-blue fur. Then they were gone.

She rubbed her eyes and looked again, nothing. There was nothing there. She must have been still sleepy. Gonsha didn't exist, probably never had, despite Xixia's tale.

The Oachnik sense of reality didn't line up with the way most humans think. Reality, fantasy and myth ran together for them, maybe it was their culture, perhaps it was the way their brains were formed.

Cassandra was far down on the definite/amorphous scale for a human, but even she felt uncomfortable with delving too deeply into Oachnik psychology. The native beings seemed to flutter in and out of everyday reality in a structureless manner. Here one minute, gone the next. Perhaps it was from generation upon generation of exposure to the divine.

Shouldering her pack, Cassandra hauled herself back to a standing position and moved on, following the others. Xixia was behind her this time. Should she tell the Oachnik about seeing the Gonsha? Maybe when they stopped to sleep and eat again. She was probably imagining it.

Again they walked through darkness. There was a lot of rock fall on the floor of the tunnel and she stumbled often, falling forward. Relieved that Samuel, the veterinarian, a huge block of a man was in front of her.

She apologized, and he replied, "The ground is very unsteady." He walked slower so as to support her. It made her feel old.

She had begun the second day of the journey tired, if it was day. She couldn't tell down in the darkness of the caverns.

They'd walked a very long time and she ended it exhausted. Managing to eat a few more dates, cheese and a handful of pistachios. Then she slid into her sleepbag and was gone.

She woke twice in the middle of the night. Once the earth was shaking beneath her. She put her arms up to cover her head, hoping nothing large would fall from the ceiling of the cavern and scrunched up into a fetal position. Nothing hit her and no one cried out, so she fell back to sleep quickly.

The second time, a child was crying. A nightmare apparently. She barely woke then.

Marita shook her gently when it was time to wake and move farther.

Cassandra drank some water and had a handful of dried cherries and more pistachios. She had to drag herself upright.

Today she felt even older than yesterday. Cassandra didn't think she'd ever walked so much in her entire life. If it wasn't so far underground she would have just stayed put. But it was, so she shoved everything into her pack, heaved it onto her back and stood swaying.

Xixia saw her and said, "You are tired. Tonight, we will be in a safer place. There will be water. We will rest for a day. The young ones and us old ones need it."

Cassandra could only nod in response, while shuffling after the others.

It seemed days later when they stopped again. Moisture hung heavily in the air. At one side of the small cavern ran an underground stream. One of the leaders tested the water and proclaimed it clean and safe. Everyone lay on the cavern floor, pushing aside the carina bushes, and hung over the rock to fill their water bottles.

When everyone had finished drinking, the Oachnik waded in and bathed themselves. Cassandra decided to do the same. She took off her boots and waded into the cool water, clothes and all. It felt almost refreshing. She slipped her socks off and rinsed them out, then wrung the water out and lay them over a large rock on the bank. Then removed the rest of her clothes and did the same with them.

Some of the other villagers followed suit, others probably concerned about nudity, declined. Cassandra was too old for that garbage.

After all her clothes were as clean as she could get by rinsing them, and her body was as clean as it could get without soap, Cassandra got out, wringing her long hair and climbed back up the bank. She retrieved the wet clothes and lay them out on a boulder by her pack. Then pulled out clean clothes and put them on without drying her skin.

It was difficult to pull the clothes on over the wet skin, she hadn't thought to bring a towel. Cassandra added a scarf and sweater. It was chilly down here, deep underground.

The water had chilled Cassandra enough that her skin felt cold. She braided her wet hair to get it out of the way. Dinner was more dates, hard cheese and pistachios, not that she was complaining, but it was going to get tiresome soon. She followed it up with a sip of her stale water. She considered dumping it out and refilling it from the stream, but was too tired to get up.

The Oachnik leaders were huddled together talking. Then they went over to speak with Xixia.

The three young ones dispersed, returning with armloads of gray, dried skeletons of dead carina bushes. They put some in a small pile in the center of the cavern and lit it. Carina was a resinous plant and burned for a very long time, giving off a scent somewhere between rosemary and lavender. It often grew in caves, not needing light because it didn't photosynthesize to live, the remarkable plants were able to get their needs met through minerals and the tiniest bit of water.

People gathered around the fire. Cassandra wasn't the only one who was cold. And the Oachnik must be chilled with their wet fur. Xixia sat down next to her.

"Would you do the honor of looking into our possible futures?"

Cassandra felt surprised.

The Oachnik had never asked her to do a reading. They'd only rarely come into the shop and usually spent their time examining herbs or crystals she'd imported. Like humans, they were attracted to the shiny.

"I would be honored." She made a move to get up, groaned at the aches in her legs and rocked back to try again.

"I'll get your cards," said Marita, bouncing up like teenager. "Where are they?"

"The interior pocket of my pack."

Marita found them and handed the bag to her.

Cassandra dusted off a place to work on the stone in front of her. She took the scarf from around her neck. Folding it into a rectangle, she spread the fabric onto the rock.

Then she removed the cards from the brightly embroidered bag and closed her eyes, inhaling a bit of smoke from the fire and clearing her mind. Letting the physical exertion of the journey drop away. Letting the stress of being surrounded by the others drain off. Letting the fear of the Caledonians flow into nothingness.

She shuffled the cards and said to Xixia, "Consider what question you would ask. When you are sure, cut the cards."

"How does one *cut* cards'?"

"Take away the top part of the deck. The card that is then on top is the beginning of the cards that have something to say to you."

Xixia widened her eyes and wiggled her whiskers in understanding.

Cassandra finished shuffling, held the cards out to her and Xixia took away the top third of the deck. Cassandra took those and returned them to the bottom of the pile, then laid out the top four cards. Three cards in a fan with the fourth card above them all.

"Would you like to share your question with those here?"

"Our question is — where do we go from here? It is a very human question."

"Indeed it is. We have: the ace of cups — ecstasy," Cassandra said. The card held a painting of a brass goblet, sitting on a rock in the middle of a fast-flowing stream. Sunlight shone down on the stream, lighting it with gold highlights which matched the complex border around the edge of all the cards.

"The four of cups—anger," she said.

The card held four, different-colored, broken and battered cups, floating down the stream, the pieces being rearranged by the dark water.

"The next is the man of worlds—achiever."

The painting on this one showed a man holding a red and yellow planet in his hands, looking at all he'd achieved.

"And the last, the key card, is the Chariot," she said.

It pictured a wild, black horse pulling a gilded chariot. The woman driving had an expression of deep concentration and her posture spoke of power and strength, golden hair flying out behind her.

"This first card is about bliss, exaltation and joy. This is our emotional abundance as it spills over and is shared with others. We have escaped. This is a fleeting experience, enjoy the grace we've been granted.

"This second card—the four of cups, is about anger. Emotions are fragile. We have been forced out of our homes, it would have come even had we stayed. We are angry about our the disruption of our lives. But we have a choice here. We can break and explode, or we can channel that anger into creative action.

"The third card—the man of worlds, is about getting things done. We have taken the first step, left our homes. Gone into the desert and safety. We must make a plan, set goals and together make it happen. This is about planning and all of us working together.

"The key card—upon which everything hinges is the Chariot. It is about constant movement, onward and upward, exploring all paths to reach our ideal. We carry our homes on our backs, at home wherever we go. But we must cultivate a sense of detachment and awareness, an inner stillness that allows us to stay centered amidst constant change. We must not run too hard or too fast, but pace ourselves for the long haul."

Cassandra looked at them and asked, " Do you have any questions?"

Magda said, "So, we've escaped and we must be happy about

that. We need to put our anger to work for us. Make a plan to oust the Caledonians. And keep moving and keep working on the plan. Any idea how to do that?"

Cassandra shook her head. She felt confused. The cards were telling them that with work, they could change the future. She'd always believed in fate. That things would be as they were destined to be.

Xixia said, "I believe that given enough time, our world will chase them away."

"How?" Cassandra asked.

"These Caledonians will not be able to live with the divine. The humans who are most rigid, break. And the Caledonians are very rigid. Those of you humans who are here, you are flexible like the talown plant. The divine came to you and you bent. You survived and adapted. The Caledonians will not be able to, that can be used against them."

"She's right," said Samuel. "We can use their brittleness against them."

"How?" asked Solshun, scratching his neck.

"It will take time," Samuel said, rubbing a hand across his face, white eyes shining out from black skin. "It will be slow. Just as our natural abilities are enhanced by the divine, so will theirs. We must work on them from a distance. Contact them by telepathy. Invade their dreams so they cannot even escape in sleep. I hate to say this, but we must push them over the edge. As many of them as we can."

"We also need to find out why they're here," said Magda. "Can we sabotage them in some way?"

"We can contact those who work on the mining operations," said Marita. "Enlist them in helping us."

"And those who stayed behind, Angel, Jake, and the others. They will be closer to them, able to help us find ways to unhinge them," Cassandra said. "Disrupt the structure of their plans."

"And your Council," said Xixia. "Can you contact any of them?"

"Perhaps," Cassandra said. "They will be more risky to contact. I expect they're being interrogated. We can't risk our being discovered."

She shifted her legs. They felt stiff and she uncrossed, straightened and recrossed them. It was then Cassandra caught a glimmer of contact with Colin. He was in darkness, imprisoned and in pain. They were torturing him to the point of unconsciousness. He was just coming awake.

"Courage," she sent him. *"You are not forgotten."* His pain made her wince as she felt the broken bones and bruises. He was thirsty, hungry and sleep deprived.

He didn't reply. Just sank back into darkness, although a little less dispirited.

What was she thinking? They couldn't help him.

"What is it?" asked Marita.

"At least one of the Council Members still on Titania, is being tortured."

"Then we begin our efforts with their guards," said Samuel.

"There will always be more guards to replace those," said Magda.

"Aim higher," Cassandra said.

"Their captain," Samuel said. "I leave the Governor to those more skilled."

"I'll take the Governor," said Xixia.

She had a gleam in her golden yellow eyes that reminded Cassandra of the vids taken of old Earth's predators. They made her shiver.

"We need to spread the word to everyone else," Cassandra said.

"I'll contact the other two groups," said Marita.

"I can touch Angel," Gene said.

"I will speak with the other Oachnik, those we are moving towards," said Solshun.

"I have a friend who's in charge of the gold mining operation at Santia," said Magda, blushing like a young woman.

Secrets, everyone had secrets.

"I will try to find out if more Council Members are here and try to speak with them, without giving away what we are doing. I don't know if they will be able to help us or not," Cassandra said.

"It is a risk," said Xixia. "One we must take."

The Oachnik kept the fire going and by the time the talking had died down, Cassandra actually felt warm and her hair was dry, although smoky.

She put the cards away and curled up in her sleepbag, falling asleep almost immediately. She woke several times throughout the night, from awful dreams of Colin screaming. Were they torturing Alexander too? The Caledonians were a backward people and had strange beliefs about sexuality. They didn't approve of any sexual partnership other than a man dominating his women.

The time to wake and move along came far too quickly.

She ate a few dates and pistachios. Then emptied and refilled her bottle with fresh water from the stream, taking a few sips.

Cassandra was finally getting used to all the walking, but that didn't make her eager to move forward. Still, she hoped they would travel to somewhere she could see the sky again. It was beautiful down here, but she missed the sunlight.

They passed deeper into the earth and she saw where the stream was in a hurry to get to. It emptied out into a large underground lake which filled up most of a cavern. The cavern felt cold, despite all her exertion. She didn't want to know what might live in such a deep, dark pool and Solshun hurried everyone past it quickly.

Then they began to climb and level out. The leaders had them refill water bottles from another stream.

"It is the last water we will find for two days," said Oncolla, a short, round Oachnik.

They climbed a bit more and then the ground leveled out again. Two of the leaders, Oncolla and Raspin went off quickly to leave the caves and hunt. Cassandra hoped they would find enough food for everyone.

They kept walking. Mile after mile. One foot in front of the other in the near darkness. Cassandra stumbled as much as she set her feet on flat rock.

There was a discussion about how to best make goat cheese between Magda and Allen which drifted back down the line to her. She tried to ignore it, but by the time they agreed to disagree, Cassandra had learned more about cheese making than she ever wanted to know.

It didn't help that her stomach was rumbling and she'd run out of salty goat cheese. She wasn't used to skipping a midday meal. The Oachnik only ate upon waking and before sleeping. None of the humans had asked the Oachnik to change the schedule. They were all in a hurry to get far away from the village. Those with young children gave them food to eat while they walked. The rest did without.

They stopped in a medium-sized cavern with a high ceiling. Four of the younger Oachnik went off to gather carina wood.

Cassandra sat on her sleepbag, chewing a date.

Oncolla followed Raspin into the cavern, they carried two poles crossing their shoulders, from which hung two large gwandyucks.

It would be a relief to eat a full meal. Cassandra's mouth watered just thinking about it.

Xixia unrolled her sleepbag and plunked down beside her, as if she were tired as well.

"The Governor, he is worried."

"You contacted him already?"

"While we walked."

"What is he worried about?"

"He did not expect New Kasbah to be emptied. He thought we would stay in our homes so they could imprison us. He doesn't know what we are doing and that worries him greatly. Also, there are problems with mining whatever they came here for. The machines they brought with them are having problems with our soil. Something about microgrit clogging up the machinery and damaging it."

Cassandra knew the mining companies here had special machinery made to deal with the small, abrasive pieces of minerals found in the soil. The Oachnik believed it was from the bones of past civilizations when this planet was a rain forest, millions upon millions of years ago.

She continued, "And he is worried about his aide and one of the Lt. Generals he brought with him. He thinks they are going to take his power and kill him."

"That one," Cassandra said. "Play that one up for him. Can you put suspicions in his mind of everything they do and say?"

Xixia cocked her head at the suggestion. "Is that how humans work?"

"Not all of us. But those who seek power often spend a great deal of energy worried about losing it."

"I will do that then. You humans puzzle me greatly."

"Many of us are very different from others. To know one human is not to know all of us. Isn't that true of Oachnik?"

"I think many Oachnik are very much the same. We do not have as many differences as you humans do."

"Many of us are from different cultures and different planets. We have very different beliefs. I definitely don't believe the same things as the Caledonians."

"If the Governor is any example of one, then for that I am grateful you are not the same."

"Thank you."

They sat in silence as the gwandyucks' meat was cut into strips, speared with sticks and roasted. The smell was almost unbearable. Cassandra put the pack over her rumbling belly, but it was so loud she could still hear it. The smoke even smelled good, almost like cooking Rosemary. It vented out through the tunnel they came into the cavern by and the one she assumed they'd go out tomorrow.

When the meat was finished cooking, it was passed around to those waiting. Cassandra held the stick and bit pieces off the hunk of meat. It was hot, greasy and smoky tasting. It was the most wonderful food she'd ever eaten. Rich and meaty.

She ate two more pieces that night before making herself stop. There was enough leftover that they'd eat it for breakfast.

She slept soundly that night and woke early. The meat was as good cold as hot. She allowed herself one sip of water, wanting to conserve it.

CHAPTER 10 - KALJU

Kalju stood on the windy plain at Mining Site 1. Lt. General Ritgan stood next to him, the hot wind blasting them both. Kalju could feel the heat even through his envirosuit.

The mining site lay just a couple hundred feet from the village of Santia. The gold miners who lived there had been drafted to help mine scillion. Most of them helped willingly, after being promised they'd get their equipment and mine back, after the Caledonians were done extracting scillion.

Those who hadn't agreed to help were killed on the spot. No second chances. Time was too short to police them. Caledonia needed scillion and needed it now.

The village was even more ramshackle than New Kasbah. It was barely functional, a few modular buildings, badly beaten by the near-constant wind and heat. Homes for about a hundred people, mostly miners, their families and a few support people. A doctor, a dentist, a food seller and the like. The village was a pathetic excuse for a community.

The flat land seemed to stretch forever, except for the small hill of mining debris that sat behind them. It was comprised of sand pulled out of the bowels of the planet. They hadn't hit rock yet, which was where the scillion would be found. This was the site where it lay the deepest, but there were the most abundant pockets here.

The drilling equipment was stuck at 150 feet deep. Again. Clogged up apparently. There was nothing to see here. Engineers running around trying to make repairs.

Lt. General Ritgan's men, standing at ease, waited for orders. Surveillance of the surrounding landscape continued, although if the planet's inhabitants were going to attack anyone, they'd need to be fast. There was no place to hide.

Ritgan seemed straightforward. A man trying to do his job well. Kalju watched as the man inwardly seethed at the obstacle. There was nothing they could do, beyond waiting.

It was time to leave. Time to go to one of the other operations. There was nothing for him to do here, he wasn't an engineer and had to trust the engineers were doing what needed to be done in order to get the machines working again.

He hated trusting people he didn't know.

"I'm sorry, Sir," said Ritgan. "The engineers fix one problem and another one appears. This is a messy business."

"We Caledonians don't like messes, do we?" asked Kalju.

"No. It's not in our nature. And colonized planets are always messy."

"Yes, they are."

"Would you like to see anything else, Sir?"

"No. Time for me to get back," Kalju said. "I need to check on Farba's progress with catching those damn villagers." Let Ritgan think he was returning to New Kasbah.

"I'll walk you to the flyer then," said Ritgan.

They walked in silence, followed by Kalju's and Ritgan's security details.

The air here had no pretense of moistness, unlike up on the butte. There the grasses were watered so there was enough moisture to keep things alive. Here, there was sand and an occasional dried clump of nearly dead brush, which might have a few brownish leaves on it. This planet was a wasteland. Why would anyone choose to live here? Gold existed on other, more pleasant, planets.

Except for the patch of land he'd flown over that was irrigated and grew date trees and a few other plants for the goats to graze. That had almost looked like paradise.

With waterways carved from stone and flowing with water. Each date palm planted within an optimal sized square and underplanted with other crops. The water flooded each square, one at a time. Life should be like that, regular and orderly. Not this sandy, rocky mess of a planet.

The sun was setting. There were no clouds to form a dramatic sunset. The sun simply disappeared beneath the horizon and was gone, a glimmer of dusk remaining and then the only light was from the work lights of the mining crew.

At the small flyer, Ritgan saluted. Then he and his men stepped back, waiting for the flyer to leave. If he was trying to unseat Kalju, the Lt. General's plans remained hidden. Unseen.

Kalju entered the small flyer, barely tall enough inside for a man to stand up right. It sat ten people. He took a seat and strapped himself in. His security detail of six followed.

"Destination, Sir?" asked the pilot.

"Mining Operation #3, but head towards New Kasbah until we're out of sight of anyone here."

"Yes, Sir."

The flyer took off smoothly, as it should on such a large, flat expanse. They flew towards the rocky crags he knew, but there was nothing to see in the darkness.

Kalju closed his eyes, but his mind wouldn't rest.

It circled the main problem. How could he hold off this rebellion he felt coming at him? It had been unwise to leave his aide, Lt. General Matif, alone with Lt. General Farba. Although he had left part of his security detail with Matif, with instructions to protect him. That way Matif couldn't dismiss them and they might be able to report back to him. But Matif wouldn't be so stupid as to do anything suspicious with a detail following him around. So that was probably a wasted effort on his part.

Farba couldn't see that Ritgan would have any part in a rebellion. He was too preoccupied with just getting the equipment up and running, and the mining started.

So far, this was just Farba. The other Lt. Generals, well, he'd wait and see what these visits turned up. The scillion better begin appearing and soon.

Or else they'd all be out of a job. Unless the other Lt. Generals could pin the problems on him. Farba wouldn't let that happen.

CHAPTER 11 - CASSANDRA

Sitting silently before the others awoke, Cassandra let her consciousness expand outward. She found Colin, he was unconscious. Touching his mind gently, she told him they were trying to help. Then she searched for other Council Members. Most of them had probably fled before the Caledonians had landed, having money and ships at their disposal.

She found only two, Aggripina and Mazin.

Aggripina had stayed because of her daughter, who was in the medical center and couldn't be moved. She was very worried about her. The Caledonians hadn't hurt her, merely imprisoned her with threats, which they hadn't acted upon yet. She was wavering as to how far she'd let them intimidate her.

Mazin had stayed because his wife had refused to leave. They had moved so many times in his long diplomatic career that this time she said, "No. I stay here. Go if you must." He didn't. And now he was stuck in Titania's main prison. The Caledonians hadn't beaten him as badly as they had Colin. He was older, perhaps they respected age. He had cooperated fully with their requests for information. Not that there was any sensitive information to give them. Still, he had many bruises and he was imprisoned. Worried about his wife and home. They had told him nothing.

Cassandra searched the prison for Alexander but didn't find him. Then she searched the temporary buildings the Caledonians had put up on the Plaza in the center of New Kasbah. In it she found Angel, Jake, Alexander and all the others who hadn't left the village.

Alexander was being cared for as the long-term cryptovirus was raging through his body. It had been rampant among space travelers five decades ago, until a vaccine was found. The cryptovirus was incurable and hid in the body, waiting for a weakness. The current situation and all its stress had opened the floodgates. The vaccine prevented people from contracting the cryptovirus, but in those already infected, it merely stopped the virus from being contagious. Those already infected were banned from all space travel — just in case. An antiquated ruling, but there were many of those.

She sent a message to Alexander. "Colin is still alive. There is hope. Recover from this. Fight it."

Then she returned to Colin and sent him a similar message about Alexander. Would it prove kinder to let both of them die without the knowledge their partner was still alive?

When she opened her eyes, everyone around her was up and packed. Ready to move on. Cassandra stood and put everything in her pack, telling them what she had learned.

Magda had contacted her friend who was pleased to help. He had some ideas. Jake, Angel and the others had been reached. Solshun had spoken with the group of Oachnik they were headed towards. They were only a few days away.

So they continued out trek through the darkness.

They were dragging themselves up a particularly rocky incline when all of a sudden Gene stopped in front of her. She bumped into him.

"Sorry," Cassandra said.

"Magda, are you all right?" Gene bent over.

Magda flailed at him.

"Answer me," he said, softly.

"Yes," she said to him. "Quiet."

She just sat there and Gene stood upright, looking around. He shrugged at her.

"No!" yelled Magda.

"What?" Cassandra asked.

"They're going against our charter. They're violating the mining ordinances and the clean water laws."

"Who?" Cassandra asked.

"The Caledonians. They've gone far beyond our own mining operations. Their equipment is up and running. Russ says their equipment spews the mining debris out on the surface of the planet and in much greater quantities than our processors. They're dumping right above the aquifers and near water above ground. They've already polluted a stream that runs into Lake Harmony."

In front of Magda, Cassandra could see Xixia. Her yellow eyes gleamed in the dim light. She was hissing in a frightening way. She didn't stop. Soon the other Oachnik joined her in hissing.

As they gathered in the tunnel, the combined lights showed their fur standing on end, sharp teeth bared, tails throttling the ground around them. Even their claws had come unsheathed.

The sight of them made Cassandra shiver. Their eyes looked somewhat glazed with the act of speaking silently either among themselves or with others of their kind, far away.

Magda, still at their feet, got up awkwardly and backed away from them.

"What will they do?" she asked.

"I have no idea. We will have to wait to see what they decide."

After a time, the Oachnik began coming back to themselves and their eyes focused on the humans.

Xixia said to Magda, "Contact your friend. Tell him not to go to work tomorrow."

Magda shook her head. "They have no choice. The Caledonians are forcing them to work."

"Do they wear uniforms?" asked Xixia.

Magda's gaze went vacant for several seconds and then she returned.

"The Titanian miners wear orange coveralls. The Caledonians wear black."

Xixia said to the other Oachnik, "Spread the word, kill the black."

Then she said to Magda, "Tell your friend to try to stay out of the way. We cannot guarantee your peoples' safety."

Magda nodded and was gone, speaking to her friend.

The Oachnik spoke among themselves using their language which Cassandra couldn't fully understand. It consisted of a series of soft groans and squeaks, gestures and postures. She wasn't even sure all the sounds were audible to human ears.

Xixia turned to the humans as nearly all the other Oachnik rushed off down the tunnel. The only remaining were Xixia, two other adults and their four young ones. Very young.

Xixia said, "They leave us now to join the other warriors. We understand this is a rash move, but clean water is the gift our world has given us. It gives us life. Unclean water gives only death. We will not allow this. I am the leader now, follow me."

"Where are we going?" Cassandra asked.

"We will rejoin the other two groups and then take you to one of our homes in the desert. I do not know how safe any of us will be after our warriors attack. The Caledonians will retaliate. Where and how, we do not know. Our people are moving under cover and spreading out into small groups so any attack will minimize the damage our enemy can do."

Cassandra nodded.

Xixia set a quick pace after that. They were all able to keep up, having spent days walking beneath the surface and getting back in shape. Still, when Xixia finally stopped for the day, Cassandra felt exhausted.

Dinner was the few pieces of leftover gwadyuck meat from the night before. It had been left on the fire all night and was chewy and the consistency of leather. The cook had salted it heavily so hopefully, it would be safe to eat for as long as it lasted. Cassandra chewed a couple of dates as well and sipped a tiny bit of water.

All the conversation was speculating about how the Caledonians might retaliate.

Cassandra looked around at the now small group. Twenty-five humans and seven Oachnik. Somehow, it didn't seem that much smaller, even though it was less than half from earlier in the day. Oachnik had a gift for being unobtrusive.

Cassandra tired of the speculation, and finally said, "We should keep to our original plan. We need to unhinge them however we can. Someone should specifically work on the Caledonians who are connected with communications at the mining site."

"I can do that." Magda smiled in a way that unnerved Cassandra.

She checked in on Colin. He was lying in his cell. Alone and in the dark, but conscious.

"I am here."

"Who are you?"

"It's me, Cassandra."

"Where are you?"

"In the desert."

"Alone?"

"No. Beyond that, best you not know."

"I've told them nothing that's not already in the Council records."

"No one would blame you if you told them more."

"There's nothing to tell. The Council has no secrets. We are transparent for a reason."

"Why are they torturing you?"

"They aren't any more, but they seem to think I'm hiding something. I'm worried about Alexander."

"He's alive."

"You know that?"

"I contacted him last night. He's sick, but alive and being cared for by friends."

"The virus?"

"Yes. Colin, we want you to help us if you are able."

"How?"

"The Caledonians are encountering the divine for the first time. The 'powers' they don't believe exist must be surfacing. Prey on that. Speak to their minds. Whisper things which will unbalance them. Do not let them know it is you. Do it when you are alone in your cell. Work on those in positions of power. Aggripina and Mazin are imprisoned as well."

"I will try."

She felt him weaken and disappear.

Cassandra contacted both Aggripina and Mazin. Neither of whom she'd ever met. They both recognized her name and didn't have enough control of their minds to keep a note of derision out of their thoughts. She didn't hold out much hope they'd be able to have any use in unbalancing Caledonians. Still she asked them to try.

"I cannot send," said Mazin. *"You're only hearing this because you're in my mind. I can hear you though."*

"Try to use that any way you can. Hear what they're afraid of and bring it up as one of your worries, reinforce it somehow."

"I'll try, but I'm afraid of being beaten."

"That's understandable. Keep yourself out of harm's way."

She felt him nod.

When she'd finished, Cassandra felt exhausted and slept.

The next day they moved rapidly even though it felt like the going was all uphill.

Cassandra walked behind Xixia. After several hours of walking, Xixia stopped to rest. Rather to let the humans rest.

"How many more days until we get where we're going?" Cassandra asked.

"If there are no blockages, tomorrow."

"Really?"

"Yes," she said.

"And will it be out in the desert, or in caves?"

"We will travel outside for part of the night. Then meet them in the caves. Caves are better for hiding. And after the attack on the mining area this morning, we must all hide."

Inwardly Cassandra groaned. Even though her house was cave-like, she appreciated the daylight and the feel of a fresh breeze on her face.

After the short rest they moved upward and came to an opening. No hidden door, just a small opening. The Oachnik squeezed through easily. Cassandra had to take her pack off and hand it out before she could get through. Others had a more difficult time, but finally, with a lot of pushing and pulling they all made it.

She stood on the hard rock, staring up at a slice the night sky. The moon of the great hare was up, which at this time of year meant it was early morning, just before dawn. She couldn't see much of the sky, the opening was between two tall rock faces that formed a narrow canyon. Barely wide enough for them to walk single file, but there was just enough moonlight and it was straight overhead, so they could see without lights.

Cassandra reveled in the fresh desert air. The scent of sand was all she smelled. The breeze was slight and the temperature perfect.

She followed the line of people and soon the canyon widened a bit. Still, they stuck fairly close to the rock walls, even though there was rubble.

Xixia had chosen the path so they could blend into the rubble and small bushes. Just in case. The canyon widened out to a large half circle.

At one point she stopped and said, "Hide."

CHAPTER 12 - KALJU

Kalju woke from a dream of fighting for his life. His heart pounded and he struggled for breath. He'd been in a room with all the Lt. Generals on the mission. They'd been unarmed and everyone was fighting. Three of them: Farba, Matif and Matton had been trying to kill him. Farba strangling him, Matif lifting his head and pounding it back down on the stone floor. Matton kicking him in the gut.

He shook himself fully awake. He was sitting upright in the flyer, strapped in. The security detail seated nearby were also napping or sitting quietly, looking out the windows.

Kalju took a deep breath, forcing his body to relax.

Three military flyers zoomed past them in the opposite direction.

"Who is that and where are they going?" asked Kalju.

The pilot contacted the other flyers.

"Sir, they're Farba's men. Chasing down the missing civilians."

"They've found them?"

"There's been a sighting, Sir. About ten miles from here."

"How close are we to Mining Camp #3?"

"We're about fifty miles away, Sir."

Had the villagers been heading to the camp? He had to make

the assumption they were. That they were trying to thwart the mission in any way possible.

He'd need to let Matton know. Increased security had already been ordered, but they had to assume the villagers were armed and ready to attack.

Part of him wanted to let Farba's incompetency ruin the entire mission. To show the Commanders that letting men rise in rank purely because of their social connections was foolish. The only thing that mattered was competency. Kalju wanted to ruin Farba, and all his kind.

His mind seized on that thought and wouldn't let go. Even though it was foolishness. He would be ruined too.

If he wasn't already, after that mess on Malion, the results of which had brought him here in the first place. He hated bureaucracy and had never wanted to be a Governor General.

He was a warrior and belonged somewhere else. Fighting. Strategizing how to overcome the enemy. The only enemies here were political and he didn't know how to fight this type of war.

He'd watched them from the sidelines, of course. Lt. Generals vying for positions and attention. Cozying up to Generals, to receive praise and advancement.

Kalju had never played that game and he didn't fully understand it. Yet here he was, not just a General, but a Governor General, with Lt. Generals looking to him for help in their quest to rise in the ranks. None of them worthy and all of them after his spot.

The one he'd worked so hard for. Not like them. Most of them were soft. Untested. He was here because he'd fought for this, hard, and won. He hadn't gamed his way into this position.

When the flyer landed, it was morning.

Mining Camp #3 camp was small. This was one of the sites that the Caledonians had found that contained scillion but wasn't being mined for gold.

It consisted of a few ramshackle buildings, hastily put up so the engineers and soldiers would have places to sleep and eat. A couple of small flyers were tied down nearby. It wasn't as windy here as out on the plains. The mountains provided a windbreak.

Matton offered them rania and some sort of flatbread with goat meat. The meat was tough and chewy. Edible, but Kalju didn't like the flavor. Perhaps it was the sauce it was cooked in, the spices.

"The spices are grown and harvested by the Oachnik," said Lt. General Matton. "Very tasty." The man licked his lips after swallowing.

Kalju nodded, but said nothing, finishing his food and rania.

His security detail ate quickly as well. Finishing before he did.

"You were hungry," said Matton, looking at all the empty plates.

Kalju nodded.

"Let me show you around," Matton said.

He led them out the door of the modular building and over to the mines. The camp was set inside a ring of jagged, rocky mountains. Dark brown and tan boulders lay here and there, attesting to the instability of the area.

Drilling was happening on the side of one of the mountains. The noise was loud enough that Matton handed them headphones to block it. There wasn't really anything to see. Several huge machines boring into the side of the mountain. Other machines coming along behind and scooping up the refuse into a third machine, which drove off to dump it.

Everything seemed to be going as planned. Matton told them they'd reached the vein of scillion just yesterday. Kalju could see the closed plastic bins being brought out. The men wearing protective gear. Scillion was toxic.

The bins were taken to a modular building set up next to a rock wall. It was camouflaged to look like part of the wall.

Matton led them over to look inside. Pallet upon pallet of scillion bins sat waiting for pickup.

"There's almost enough to ship back to Caledonia. We've called for a transport ship. Should be here tomorrow," said Matton. "The engineers think this deposit is larger than they initially thought."

The man grinned, as if he'd discovered a new perfectly habitable planet.

Kalju said, "Very good. How much larger?"

"Three, maybe four times larger, Sir."

"That might just make up for the lack of scillion at Camp #1."

"They're not finding it?" asked Matton, eyebrows raised in surprise.

"They can't get the machinery working. Microgrit."

"Oh, that's right. They're digging in pure sand for the first couple hundred feet. Solid rock is easier."

The tour ended, they went back into the food building. As they entered the door, Kalju caught sight of one of the cooks talking with an Oachnik.

"You have natives here?" he asked.

"Oh, that's Xaxian. She's the one who we get spices and meat from."

"A native?"

"Yes, she's harmless. We test everything for toxins. She takes some of the mens' memorabilia in return. Especially fond of jewelry—rings, ear rings are so popular these days. And the food she brings us is wonderful. Better than the standard stuff that's shipped from Caledonia. The men are all tired of that."

So, Matton was going native. That's why he was so excited about the large deposit of scillion. Kalju had seen his type. He'd be difficult to get off planet when the mission was over. Might not come at all, but disappear into the caves, like the villagers. In the meantime, his command would degenerate into a mess of native lawlessness and lack of discipline.

He'd have to send a report back about another Lt. General. In the meantime, Kalju would have to make sure the mining stayed on task, the warehouse was filling up and the scillion was being shipped off to Caledonia.

Another Lt. General to babysit.

CHAPTER 13 - CASSANDRA

They hid where they could. People flattening themselves against the rock. Cassandra crawled under a scratchy carina bush. Not much cover.

A few minutes later, she heard a small flyer crossing the canyon slowly. If they were Caledonian soldiers, they'd have night vision equipment.

Cassandra looked at Xixia. Her eyes had that distant look to them. She was communicating with someone.

The flight circled the canyon, following the top edge, but not dipping down. It was on the far side of the canyon when the flyer suddenly turned and flew straight towards them, shooting.

Their guns shot up rows of sand before they got closer. Were they trying to herd the group? Trying to get them to move?

"Follow me!" yelled Xixia. "To that dark space. There's a door."

She pointed at a dark point on the canyon wall far in front of them. They'd have to run across the middle of the canyon to get there.

Xixia sprinted.

Cassandra followed as fast as she could, which wasn't that fast. The others did as well. Many of them passed her.

The flyer kept shooting at them. People screamed.

Cassandra didn't stop. Couldn't breathe. Just kept running.

Her side hurt. She kept running.

They poured in through the hole in the rock wall, and kept moving. Someone had a light and Cassandra could see dim shapes moving away from the opening. There was rubble everywhere.

She twisted her ankle on a large stone that flipped when she stepped on it. Fell. Got up again, hobbled farther to get out of the way.

Then collapsed in a heap on a pile of rocks.

Cassandra didn't know if she passed out or not. When she could breathe again, Marita was gently touching her shoulder.

"Cassandra, are you all right?"

"Twisted my ankle." Her side still hurt. She thought it had been a stitch in her side from running. But when she felt it, it still hurt. "My side hurts. It feels wet, but that could be sweat. Or did I get hit?"

Marita shone a light on her side. The woman's reaction told Cassandra that yes, she was bleeding.

"I'll get Samuel to look at you."

"Did anyone else get shot?"

"Many people did. Some didn't make it to the cave. We can't go back out. The flyer's parked on the canyon wall. Just waiting."

"They'll send for more flyers. Someone will land down here and follow us into the cave," Cassandra said.

"No. Xixia's going to blow the opening as soon as she can."

"She has explosives?"

"The Oachnik are full of surprises."

Marita helped her shrug the pack off.

Samuel came over and said, "Well now, what have you done to yourself?" His deep voice sounded melodic. He poked and prodded, moving her shirt around. Then washed the wound with some water.

"The bullet just grazed you. You are very lucky." He dried the wound and then put something cold and stinging on it that felt like a bandage.

"She said she twisted her ankle too," said Marita.

"Right or left?"

"Left," Cassandra said.

He lifted her leg and touched it gently, pivoting the lower leg at the knee. He touched the leg in several places until she said, "Ow, right there."

He felt it some more, pressing harder. "It's a sprain, I think. It will hurt. I have no ice and you can't keep it elevated, we've got to move on as soon as possible. About all I can do is to wrap it and give you a pain killer. Someone will have to take your pack or you can leave it behind. If you can find a cane, a walking stick, it will help."

Not likely. Cassandra felt sure there were sticks aplenty out in the canyon, but not here in the caves.

He wrapped the ankle and gave her a pill to take, which she did promptly.

Cassandra sat up, wincing at the pain in her side.

Marita helped haul Cassandra to her feet. With Marita's help, Cassandra hobbled over to a boulder and sat down to wait until everyone was ready. She put the sore ankle up on another boulder to elevate it a bit while it was possible. It wasn't above her heart, but it would have to do.

"I'll carry your pack when it's time," said Marita. "I'm strong enough." She plonked it down next to Cassandra and went back to helping people.

All the Oachnik had made it into the cave, they were much faster than humans. It looked like one of the young ones had hurt an arm. She wore a white bandage just above her wrist.

Most of the humans were either sitting on rocks, laying on the ground or helping. Cassandra began counting. There were four on the ground. Five helping and ten sitting. And herself.

That meant five people were still out in the canyon. She hoped they were all dead, because what the Caledonians would do to them would be worse.

Cassandra tried to see faces. Samuel, Marita, Allen and two

others with their backs to her were helping. Magda sat on a nearby rock, as did Sara. Their faces looked full of sadness.

I touched Magda's arm. "Who is still outside?"

"Gene. Gene was shot. He must be dead. Kara, Quinn, Maxine were shot. Tad is out there too."

"Can anyone tell if they're still alive?"

"None of them have moved. If they're alive, it's not by much," said Sara. She shifted her head in such a way that one of the lights hit it and Cassandra could see streaks of tears.

Xixia came to them and said, "I am afraid we must leave them. As soon at we can move, we must. I can collapse this part of the cave once all of you have left it. But there are other entrances. They will find one. We must be long gone and we can't move very quickly."

She was right.

"We will do what we must," Cassandra said.

Magda nodded in response.

Sara just looked at those on the floor, "We'll probably need stretchers for some."

"How?" Cassandra asked.

"We'll need sturdy poles."

Xixia said, "Come with me." She motioned to one of the other Oachniks to follow her.

They moved off down a tunnel.

"Bring me a cane if you find one," Cassandra yelled after them.

It wasn't long before she and Sara returned with eight long, straight poles and one short one.

Sara tossed the short one to Cassandra. It even had a bend on one end to make a nice hand rest.

Sara and a couple of the others found a way to secure sleepbags between two poles. Then the four injured people were slid into them. With one person on each end, the stretchers could be carried down the tunnels. The people who weren't carrying stretchers were carrying extra packs. Except for Magda and Cassandra. It was all they could do to haul themselves along.

They set off following the Oachnik with the youngsters. Once all of them had left the main cavern, they heard Xixia set off her explosives. The ground shook and small pieces of rock and debris fell from the ceiling of the tunnel above them.

Upon rejoining then, Xixia said, "They are here. They brought five flyers. When it is daylight, they will find the other openings. We must move away from our final destination or we will run into them."

"How many more days?" Cassandra asked.

"We only had one more day, now we will have four."

"We don't have food."

"Gwala and I will need to hunt. And we must find water soon again."

"And we must rest. We've been walking all day. Even without injuries. . . ."

"Yes, we must rest. But we must go deeper first."

Cassandra sighed. Grateful that she'd had a few lungfuls of the cool night air.

They seemed to move on down into the darkness forever. Her ankle throbbed even with the painkiller. She felt glad for the cane and used it to keep herself upright.

Up ahead of her, people periodically shifted who was carrying the stretcher and who carried the extra packs. Marita came back and let Cassandra lean on her for a time, which helped a lot.

The air grew earthier smelling. Like good damp soil that Cassandra had smelled once inside one of the produce greenhouses.

"Water," said Xixia, her mouth widening in a grin.

The dampness speeded everyone up. They entered into a large cavern with a stream cutting through one side.

Xixia said, "We rest and sleep here."

Samuel and the others helped the four people out of the sleepbags, so he could examine them.

Mia, Daniel, Luna and Eli were the four who'd been shot badly. Mia made clothes and sold them. Daniel worked at one of the farms. Luna was a geologist who worked with the miners. Eli was a teacher. Several others had been shot, but could still walk. They'd all need to rest for a long time tonight.

As soon as everyone was settled, Xixia and Gwala left to hunt. Cassandra had no idea where they found the energy to even walk.

While the hunters were gone, the others refilled all the water bottles after the water was tested. Then everyone who could lay down and rested. Samuel gave Cassandra another painkiller and she used the pack to raise her ankle. It was badly swollen, even with the wrapping he'd done.

Samuel didn't sleep. She watched him sit by Mia and listen to her moan. She had a fever from her wounds. Marita told Cassandra that of the four of them, Mia was doing the worst.

At some point during the night, Xixia and Gwala returned with two great hares. What they called hares were the size of a medium goat with two rows of sharp teeth. Their only resemblance to the hares of old earth were the huge ears and the hopping. Great hares lived in the canyons, preying on lizards, mice and birds.

CHAPTER 14 - KALJU

Kalju stood staring at the disarray that was Camp #2. The equipment had been up and running for days now. Excavating a massive amount of stone, and very little scillion, apparently.

Clouds of dust hung in the air and he could smell iron, and even a hint of moisture.

"We know it's here. We've checked and double checked the readings," said Lt. General Yutif, his uniform in the same wrinkled disarray as the camp. "We just haven't found it yet."

This camp had stony rocks on opposite sides. Not tall enough to be mountains, but fairly large all the same. The debris pile was dumped near a river. This was one of the few areas of the planet with water on the surface.

It was a miracle there hadn't been a village built here. There had however, been a group of biologists who had been chased away. Yutif had their shacks torn down and equipment destroyed.

Now the debris was leaching radioactive chemicals into the river. Kalju had heard the complaints before he left to visit the camps. One of the biologists had reached New Kasbah, to complain.

"It's a fragile area, but one that supports more life than the rest of the planet put together. There are fish we still haven't named.

Mammals and birds that exist nowhere else in this universe. All we're asking is that they dump the mining debris away from the river. Water is such a precious thing on this planet," the sunburnt, blistered man had said.

Kalju said he'd look into it, but promised nothing.

He really didn't care about this pathetic heap of rock. It had no value. Right now, only the scillion was worth anything, and only because Caledonia wanted it. Should another weapon be invented tomorrow that didn't use scillion, even that would be worthless.

Nearly half of one of the hills had been run through the processing equipment and dumped alongside the river. He doubted if the Commanders would care either.

It would have been a simple thing to dump it elsewhere. But to have to use the equipment to move it now, well, there was just no time. It wasn't worth the effort. What had the biologist been thinking?

What the problem was, that they'd found so little scillion. Had the initial survey been wrong?

"Is this the right location?" asked Kalju

"The engineers and geologists tell me it is. The survey can't pinpoint locations exactly, but our equipment tells us there's scillion here. There's still a chance that the bulk of it's in the un-mined half of this hill. And we haven't begun working on the other one yet," said Yutif.

The man was certainly an optimist.

The tour was short, there wasn't much to see and it was too damn hot with no wind at all. He felt drenched even in the envirosuit. It was black, because all Caledonian uniforms were black. Black the color that included everything, because Caledonia was the universe.

The air felt still. The only sounds were the roaring, grinding machinery and the rushing river.

His wristband pinged and he held it up to read a message from Farba.

"Villagers found. Have killed many of them. Seeking out the rest."

What did that mean? Seeking out the rest? If he found them, why was he seeking them? And why had he killed them? They might be able to tell him what mining site they were intending to sabotage.

The problem with delegating was that one risked the incompetency of others. Farba was incompetence personified.

Well, one more camp to see and then he'd go back to the Council headquarters and see if Farba had cleaned up his botched-up chaotic disaster.

"Let's go over to the mess. Today, we've got some gazelle steaks we brought from Caledonia."

"You brought gazelle steaks?" Kalju raised his eyebrows, and his mouth began to water at the thought of roasted gazelle.

"The engineers and miners aren't like soldiers. They're not used to deprivation and they don't work well under those conditions. They're soft. I've found they work best when catered to. So, yes, I brought gazelle steaks. And wine from Cabrya. It's not like we didn't have to import food anyway. We didn't bring hunters with us. My soldiers need to focus on mining and keeping this camp safe from any interlopers."

"I think we'll stay for dinner," said Kalju, wishing he'd thought ahead and brought better food from Caledonia. He was a soldier and it was hard to admit he relished good food. His ability to withstand deprivation was a matter of pride, but his security detail would appreciate the break from standard rations. And he could learn more about Yutif, who was clearly a very smart leader.

In the end, it was a very good plan. During the meal, he learned Yutif wouldn't be part of a plan to overthrow him. He wasn't the backstabbing sort. He'd come at Kalju from the front, and with warning. He wouldn't collude with the other Lt. Generals. He wanted everything for himself. He'd treat those who assisted him well, although they were beneath him, not his equal.

Yutif was the most dangerous of them all.

They returned to the flyer and flew to Camp #4.

Kalju slept on the way there, making use of his time. They

would fly through the night and it was better than stewing on all the possible plots to sabotage his mission.

When he woke, the sun was coming up on the horizon. The small village of Naritana and Mining Camp #4 lay beneath the flyer.

The mining equipment was not at work, but it had clearly carved a chunk out of the nearby rock, although that could be old work done by the gold miners.

Naritana had a population of maybe seventy-five people, all humans. They were either gold miners, miners' families, or support for them. Medical, food suppliers, that sort of thing. The village had been built in the shade of tall red cliffs. Short stone buildings, some had even been carved into the lower cliff face, stood nearby. The stone would be cooler to live in.

Still, all in all, it was another ugly little village. He hated this planet.

The flyer landed on the far edge of the village, at the refueling station. There was no place to land near the mining operation. Who had thought that out? That meant the scillion, and the gold before it, would need to be moved through the village to be transported anywhere.

Lt. General Lassorn had obviously been tipped off they were coming. He came out to meet the flyer himself.

"Governor General Kepa," he said, saluting.

Kalju returned the salute as he exited the flyer.

"What brings you to our small part of Titania 37?"

"I just wanted to see all the mining camps. See how things were going for myself. I can only glean so much from others' reports," he said, smiling and playing the convivial leader. "I'm not good at sitting around and waiting."

They walked through the streets of the village, red dust rising from the crushed stone underneath their feet. The sound of all the boots crunching would have warned the entire village of their presence. He looked around at his security detail.

They were already on high alert. Aware of their surroundings, hands on their weapons.

They followed Lassorn through the village. Kalju half listened as the man chattered on like a grayling trying to win a mate. The man obviously loved to talk.

Talking was a tactic that many used successfully as a decoy. What was the man hiding? Or was he stalling? And for what?

The hair on the back of Kalju's neck stood upright. He switched his full body armor on, hoping Lassorn wouldn't hear it. He wanted to see how this played out. He'd need proof of incompetency or treason for the Commanders.

His security detail heard his armor switch on and did the same with theirs. They moved into high alert mode. He knew one of them was contacting the pilot. He hoped the pilot had followed protocol. They might need to leave quickly.

Tension ran down his back and he breathed deeply to make it release. None of this felt right.

He caught a glint of sunlight off metal on one of the rooftops. Could have been a gun. Could have been a civilian watering their garden. These people grew food on their roofs. Silly notion.

Danip, one his detail was looking at him. Kalju moved his eyes ever so slightly. Danip passed the message onto the others.

Kalju only had a handgun. He hadn't expected trouble. He'd be next to useless in any sort of gunfight, but he could deal with Lassorn if the man didn't get his armor up in time. Although he suspected Lassorn was prepared for what was coming up.

The mine, they would attack them in the mine. Where there were fewer witnesses. Unless the villagers were in on it. Had Lassorn gone that far?

Only seconds had passed since he'd put his armor up. He needed to take charge of the situation. Do the unexpected.

Kalju pressed a button on his wristband that made it sound like a message was coming in.

"Excuse me," he said. He stopped walking and looked at the wristband, pretending to read it.

He swore.

"I need to return to New Kasbah. There's an urgent situation that needs dealing with. I'm afraid I'll have to tour your mine another time, Lt. General."

The man stood staring, his mouth gaping open as if to collect insects. Then closed it.

Lassorn said, "But Sir, it won't take long . . ." The man mumbled on, grasping for straws.

Kalju recognized the signs of someone who's carefully laid plans had been upset.

He nodded to his detail, turned and jogged back to the flyer without event.

There were four armed men of Lassorn's outside the flyer, but the flyer door was closed, as it should have been. One of the men was speaking into his wristband.

The other three saluted.

Tarune, one of his security detail and one of the largest men Kalju had ever seen, stood in front of the soldier talking into his wristband. He towered over the man.

"You'll be wanting to salute the Governor General."

The man looked panicked and hastily saluted.

The man nodded to the others and they drew back from the flyer. The pilot opened the door when messaged and his face drooped in relief.

"Take off now," said Kalju.

"Yes sir," said the pilot, flicking switches.

They strapped in and the flyer took off.

"Do you know what that was about, Sir?" asked Tarune.

"No, I don't, but it sure didn't feel right."

"No, it didn't," said Danip.

"It was a trap, Sir," said Justane. "Look, there's a platoon there by the mine. Gathered around and listening to the Lt. General."

Kalju looked at the crowd gathering around Lassorn. Fully armed men were still emerging. Miners came from the rocks. There were also soldiers on the roofs at the end of the village near the mines.

Villagers, too, were streaming towards the mines.

A large blast came from below and Kalju realized it was a rocket launcher.

"Evade," he yelled at the pilot. "Incoming fire."

The flyer swooped upwards and the movement pinned Kalju back into his seat.

Through his window, he watched as the rocket streamed past, narrowly missing them. It continued on its trajectory. It was old weaponry then. Not one that would track them.

Lassorn was going to pay for this.

Once they'd gotten far enough away from the camp and his adrenaline blast subsided, Kalju tried to figure things out.

His best guess was that Lassorn had deserted and the miners had paid him off. Bought him. There was no mining going on, other than gold. Or perhaps these miners were responsible for selling the scillion that had caught Caledonia's attention to begin with. He needed to inquire if Command knew what mine that scillion had come from.

He got a message from Lt. General Ritgan that his camp was under attack by the Oachnik. They had targeted the Caledonians, leaving the miners alone. Half his men had been killed before the Oachnik were driven off. His men had chased them for a while, but they melted into the desert and disappeared. Equipment was damaged and would need to be repaired.

Damn. Another setback.

Kalju sat back in his seat and sipped some water, The cold and clean taste refreshed his mouth and he sat back in his seat. Thinking.

Then it struck him. What if Lassorn, and possibly some of the others, had been on a different mission? What if command had decided to get rid of him, after the disaster on Malion? They'd found a convenient way. Put him on this backwater planet, let him flounder. Give him two or three inept Lt. Generals to help mess things up. Add in a revolution by the natives. Then have one of the Lt. Generals rebel and kill him any way possible.

Would the Commanders do such a thing?

Of course they would. If it rid them of a troublesome officer they didn't want to see rise any higher. It would serve as a test for the Lt. Generals. See which ones they could really trust and which ones were truly ineffective and incompetent.

How was he going to get out of this mess?

CHAPTER 15 - CASSANDRA

WHEN CASSANDRA WOKE, THERE WAS A FIRE GOING AND THE SMELL OF roasting meat reminded her she'd gone to sleep without eating the night before.

Sitting up quickly, she remembered the gunshot wound as well as the bloody ankle. She yelped in pain.

Samuel came over and said, "Serves you right. Don't move so fast." He unwrapped her ankle and then wrapped it up tighter. "Well at least some of the swelling has gone down. Let's look at your side."

Cassandra pulled the shirt up and he ripped the bandage off quickly, which made her yelp again.

"It's healing well. I'll put another bandage on, but treat it gently today. It might be the last bandage I can spare."

"I'm glad you came so well prepared."

"So am I. I had no idea I'd need so many. I knew Thomas wouldn't be coming and we weren't bringing livestock, but I didn't plan on this," he said, gesturing to all the injured.

Thomas was New Kasbah's only doctor. Samuel was the veterinarian. The Council had another doctor, up on their hill, but he wouldn't see any of the villagers.

Thomas had been severely injured in his youth and walked

with the help of machinery. Machinery which didn't work that well in sandy deserts. He'd declined to come, saying those who were staying were the elderly and ill and needed his help more.

Samuel gave Cassandra another painkiller and helped her up. He handed her the cane. Cassandra sipped some water and wobbled over to the fire, wincing. She'd be glad when the painkiller kicked in. Her side felt better, but the ankle hurt like hell. She felt sure it would only be worse by the end of the day. Whose bandage had she gotten, a goat's?

Xixia and Gwala were sleeping. Misrana the other adult Oachnik was cooking and watching all four youngsters at the same time.

She grinned at Cassandra and said, "Here, take my knife and cut off a strip like so for yourself."

Cassandra watched as she cut off a strip of the hot meat and handed it to the young one with the bandaged arm.

She took the knife and did the same, finding a place to hold the meat that didn't burn her fingers.

It was greasy and strong tasting meat. More gamey tasting than goat meat. She quite liked it, especially since her stomach was grumbling.

"This is wonderful. Thank you."

Misrana nodded at her and went back to portioning out meat to the youngsters.

A few people were up, most still sleeping.

After finishing the meat, Cassandra dragged her sleepbag up onto a boulder and spread it out. Then she lay down again, but this time she'd be able to get up alone.

She wasn't going to bother to change clothes, even though the shirt had a hole in it now and was crusted with dried blood. She wasn't about to go swimming and clean up. Not with the bad ankle. No one would care. They all smelled pretty ripe.

She curled up in her sleepbag and went back to sleep. When she woke everyone else was finally up. After eating more hare and packing some away for later, Marita helped her stuff the sleepbag in the pack. They all refilled their water, then moved out. Marita supported Cassandra for as long as she could, then rested. Then came back and offered her arm again.

They were still carrying four stretchers. Eli, Luna and Daniel were partly awake. Apologizing for inconveniencing everyone when they weren't sleeping. Mia was still moaning and crying out in her sleep.

Cassandra could tell Samuel was very worried about Mia. He looked exhausted and she wondered if he'd slept at all.

They didn't move as quickly today, but more surely and deliberately. Everyone was tired what with carrying stretchers and extra packs. They kept going down into the depths of the planet. Xixia would pause sometimes and look vacant. Cassandra assumed she was speaking with someone, asking which way to go. Leading everyone away from the surface caves where the Caledonians might be looking for them.

She asked Xixia when they stopped for water and a snack, "Are you in touch with other Oachnik?"

"Yes," she said. "They are leading the Caledonians into traps and killing them. They will never be found."

"Aren't they wearing equipment that can be tracked?"

"I'm sure they are. That will be destroyed. But it means the place we were originally headed to will have to change. Soon these caves will be crawling with the offworlders."

"Which means we've got a longer trek ahead of us."

"Yes, it does. But what did your cards say? We are the Chariot. We carry our homes with us and keep moving."

"I hope I survive to see that."

"The second day of an injury is always the worst. You will heal and grow stronger."

Mostly, they walked on in silence.

Cassandra spent the time arguing with herself. Trying to think of tactics to use on the Caledonians in an attempt to keep her mind off pain in the ankle.

And ignore the fear. The Caledonians were above them somewhere. And they'd kill them if they could.

They walked silently, there was no singing during this part of the trek.

She grieved for the loss of Kara, who'd always had a kind word for everyone. For Quinn, who helped Cassandra repair her refrigeration unit last year. For Tad, who she hadn't really known, but who many said was a gifted mechanic. For Maxine, who always went out of her way to say hello to her, even when going out of her way had seemed difficult for her. Lastly, for Gene, who could always be counted on to help anyone with anything he could. He'd been a very kind man. Cassandra hoped that all of them were actually dead and not captured by the Caledonians. She hoped they'd died quickly.

Cassandra worried about Colin. She couldn't reach him or the others. It might be that she was simply too tired, or that her body was too weighed down with everything right now. It might be they were all asleep. Cassandra hoped it was temporary and that when it was time to rest, she'd be able to speak with them again.

She tried to contact any Caledonians. For a time she was able to hear one of them. He'd become separated from the main group somehow. There was something about the damn natives having attacked them. He was wandering in tunnels and caverns. His coms wouldn't function down there, so he was completely alone. Then she felt his terror as he faced a huge creature with bluish white fur, sharp teeth and claws. He was gone after that. Dead, she hoped.

Had it been an Oachnik, who attacked him? Or could it really have been a Gonsha? She'd never gotten around to telling Xixia about the sighting she'd had, thinking it had probably been one of those things one sees on the edges of sleep and waking. Things that aren't real.

When they moved into a larger tunnel, Cassandra moved up farther in the line until she found Xixia.

"Xixia, I was in the mind of a Caledonian wandering the caves. He was attacked by what looked like a Gonsha."

Xixia looked at her, head cocked and teeth bared.

"And days ago, when we stopped for a break in a cavern, I ate, then fell asleep. When I woke, I saw three Gonsha up near the roof of the cavern. Just for an instant, then they were gone. I meant to tell you, but things happened. I didn't know if I'd dreamt it or if it was real, but now. ..."

"You dreamt it," she said, her voice grating as if tension squeezed her vocal cords. "The Gonsha are all dead."

"But what if they're not?"

"No. They are dead. What the Caledonian saw was not real either. Perhaps one of my people put it into his mind."

"Perhaps," Cassandra said, unconvinced.

At any rate, the rigidness of Xixia's posture told her subject was closed.

The four days passed in monotonous walking through the near darkness, one foot in front of the other. Her side healed, but the ankle didn't. It needed rest. Samuel told her. Finally, Eli was healed enough to walk and Samuel made Cassandra lie in a stretcher, ankle above her heart, all day while others carried her.

She felt terribly embarrassed.

Finally, Lucas said, "Please stop apologizing. It's really annoying. Just be quiet, heal and enjoy the ride."

"You're right," she said. "I'm being a jerk."

Marita still carried her pack.

"At least it's lighter," said Marita, teasing her. "There's no food left in it."

Cassandra learned to shut up and lay back, watching the ceiling of the tunnels and caverns go by. She slept off and on. She tried to reach out to Colin and the others, but couldn't. She really did need rest and took it.

Samuel made her ride in the stretcher for two and a half days. By then Luna was up and walking again. Mia had returned to consciousness, but was still very weak from blood loss. Daniel was healing, but his injury was in his thigh. He wasn't ready to walk again.

Samuel began to sleep through the night and his smiles came more easily again. The weight of all the injuries had been such a strain on him.

When Cassandra began walking again, her ankle was much, much better and only ached at the end of the day. She still slept with it elevated, even though Samuel said it wasn't necessary any longer. And still kept it wrapped during the day.

One day, Cassandra realized she didn't need the cane anymore. She kept it, and used it in the rough, rocky places, mainly because it felt like she could use it as a handy weapon if needed. It was hard wood and might be useful. Having a hand wrapped around the smooth wood made her feel stronger.

They continued to walk, long past the four days. Cassandra carried the pack and they were down to two stretchers, which gave the stretcher carriers more of a chance to rest. They began to pick up speed as people recovered from their injuries.

It seemed forever before they began to head upwards again. Cassandra felt such relief when they entered a cavern one day and sun peeked in through holes in the walls.

They all stopped and were completely silent. The sun was the first thing she noticed.

Then Cassandra saw the houses. They were built of carved stone with doorways covered with decorated animal hides. There was not a surface of the cavern left undecorated in some way. Her brain reeled, trying to make sense of it all. The houses were decorated in such a way that the they were hidden by optical illusions. The cavern was flooded by color and design.

"This was our original destination. My people have fled to another of our villages," said Xixia. "This one is known to the people in New Kasbah, and to the Caledonians, we must assume."

"It's so beautiful," said Mia, sitting up.

"We will rest here," said Xixia. "Spend one night. Then we must continue on. They will have left some stored food behind."

Xixia and Misrana began to enter the houses, searching for stored food. Gwala took the youngsters to another cave, all of them carrying empty clay containers to bring back water.

The rest of them put their packs down around the fire pit.

Cassandra stared at the fire pit. Was it safe to build a fire? The sun was visible inside the cave, fire could probably be seen from the outside.

Xixia returned with a large container and a huge grin on her face.

"Our luck has turned, as you humans would say. Build a small fire."

"Is that safe?" Cassandra asked.

"We will cook while it is light. Then put the fire out."

Cassandra nodded and continued pulling the sleepbag out of her pack. Lucas and Sara had already leapt to bringing over the firewood which had been stored nearby.

Cassandra sat down on the sleepbag, removing her boots and unwrapped the ankle. Then massaged it. The area above it wasn't swollen anymore and both ankles looked the same. The injured one wasn't even tender. She decided it was healed and wouldn't wrap it again. Cassandra rolled up the wrap and tucked it into the pack. Just in case it was needed in the future.

Misrana and Xixia made some sort of stew out of kiliya, a native grain, and dried etalia strips. It contained the sweet, dried root of the lebtya plant and chopped, dried dates, plus spices Cassandra had no names for. It was incredibly delicious.

Xixia took a bite of it, closing her eyes as a slow smile spread across her face.

"This is wonderful," Cassandra said, to both of them.

"It is a favorite meal of our people," said Misrana. "Few humans have ever had it. We don't eat it often in the village. We do not have the right spices and kiliya is difficult to find. It takes paying careful close attention to the plants. The seeds must be harvested at just the right time. As often as not the etalia get them before we do."

"I am honored to have tasted it."

The light outside was dimming.

"Time to put the fire out," Cassandra said.

"It is so," said Xixia.

The youngsters scooped sand from the cavern floor and the beautiful cavern walls dimmed. They finished their meals in near darkness.

"Can we do another reading?" asked Mia.

"Not tonight," said Xixia. "Sound travels too readily through the open cavern walls. We will have to wait until we are in a smaller, more secluded space."

So they slept, their bellies full for the first time in days. Except for two of the Oachnik, who stood guard.

In the morning, Xixia and Gwala searched the rest of the village's stores and added a few things to everyone's packs. They refilled the water bottles and packed up.

Then Xixia led them down another tunnel that went down to another level. They moved quickly now. There was only the one stretcher to carry as Daniel was walking again. Mia was healing fast now, but Samuel wouldn't let her walk for more than a quarter of the time.

Xixia appeared to know this cave system better than the ones they'd been in previously. She didn't hesitate at crossroads the way she had before.

The Oachnik were hunting every day now. Lucas and Eli following them, trying to learn their techniques and failing. Oachnik were much faster than humans with claws and sharp teeth as weapons. Although Lucas and Eli had knives, they weren't fast enough to catch much. Mostly, they just watched from what they told Cassandra.

They were deep enough in the cave system to make fires to cook the meat. Every now and then Xixia would ask for something she'd put in one of the packs and she'd add that to the meat, making it taste incredible. The Oachnik spices tasted rich and earthy, giving the meat a depth of taste it was missing on its own.

Cassandra still tried to contact Colin with no luck. Magda had been unable to contact her friend, Russ. Samuel said he caught a glimpse of Jake's mind, but it felt confused, almost delirious. No one else had any success contacting any human, even the Caledonians.

One night, Cassandra asked Xixia how she was doing.

Xixia said, "I can still speak with other Oachnik, but cannot find the Caledonian Governor."

"Are the other groups all right?" asked Magda.

"Yes, they are already at our destination. They weren't attacked by the Caledonians."

Cassandra felt relieved by that. And guilty that she hadn't even wondered about where they were. She'd been so busy worrying about the group she was with.

"How long until we get there?" asked Marita.

"Tomorrow. We should be there tomorrow."

"Where is it?" asked Mia.

"It is one of our villages. We call it Gwasanda, it means refuge. It was where we met and regrouped during the war with the Gonsha. It is much like the village we just left, except it is entirely enclosed. There are nearby tunnels leading outside which are guarded, but the main village is protected by strong stone. It is larger than the village we just left."

Cassandra felt relieved to be so close. She hoped they could make it there soon. And be able to go outside. She longed to feel the sun on her skin. Such a simple thing. Humans weren't meant to be subterranean.

She finished the roasted meat and licked her fingers, having given up the concept of cleanliness. She longed for a bath, even in a cold stream. One of these days. Maybe even in a day or two. She stank. But then so did everyone around her.

Cassandra slept then, soundly. She didn't remember her dreams, but the Gonsha were in it. Ripping humans to shreds.

CHAPTER 16 - KALJU

THE FLYER MADE IT BACK TO NEW KASBAH IN THE EARLY HOURS OF the morning. Kalju went straight up to the Council meeting room and closeted himself in. The room smelled sandy, just like the rest of the planet. It felt stuffy. He opened one door, cracking it enough to let the cool night air inside. The guard outside saluted him and Kalju returned the salute.

The security detail who had been with him had gone to sleep and been replaced by another part of the detail. Kalju ordered the security on the Council Complex doubled and on high alert. Lt. General Farba and his men had long ago taken up residence in the village.

Kalju gave a planet-wide order that all the large weapons the Caledonians had brought with them to Titania 37 were to be brought to the Council Complex for safe storage.

The weapons had been intended as defense against rebelling settlers, not to be used by them, or those they had turned to their cause.

This would leave the mining camps without immediate protection. They would still have their individual weapons. That would have to be enough.

Large weapons like the rocket launcher wouldn't be much help against guerrilla forces like rebelling colonists anyway. The individual weapons could do a lot of damage if they were close enough.

Few of Caledonia's flyers were armed. He ordered those to return to their base here.

Kalju made sure his own flyer was armed. His third security detail was seeing to that now. Adapting the weapons already here at the Complex.

He wouldn't get caught out again.

Kalju paced around the near-empty room, his shoes thumping on the stone floor, echoing footsteps. Keyed up like he always was before battle. This was a different type of battle.

He sent out a message to Lt. Generals Ritgan, Matton, Farba and Yutif about the attack on his flyer by Lt. General Lassorn. He wanted to give them fair warning. Just in case any of them weren't in on this treason.

What if the Oachnik attack on Camp #1 hadn't really happened? What if Ritgan, finding that Lassorn had failed to kill him, was trying to lure him out?

He sent a carefully worded message to Lassorn, inquiring about the rocket that had narrowly missed his flyer. Saying he was sure it was a mistake. And for Lassorn to prove it was, he would need to comply with the maintenance crew coming to pick up their large weapons.

He would speak to his aide, Lt. General Matif, in person and relay all this. Get his reaction and decide if he should distance himself further from the man.

He sipped more rania. It would not help him sleep, and he badly needed sleep. There was no time. Too much to do while he waited to see who complied with his orders. He was starting a sequence of events that there could be no stopping now.

Just before daylight came, he gathered his detail and all his men who were in the complex, about two hundred. They met outside, at the foot of the butte.

He climbed up the shiny slickness of a flyer and stood atop it, looking out over them. It was warming up already, the tang of metallic soil on the breeze. His mouth felt dry from the bitter rania he drank all night long.

The sun rose over the horizon, casting everything in a golden orange color. Except the black uniforms of his men. His men. It was times like this Kalju was truly proud to be a soldier. A Caledonian.

"Men of Caledonia, my brothers in arms, we have a situation here. We come to this planet on a peaceful mission, to extract scillion for our weapons. But there is a worm loose among us."

The crowd murmured. The rumor had already made its rounds then.

"As we were leaving one of the mining camps yesterday, we were fired upon. From our own. I don't know how many of our people are involved, but at least one has gone over to the enemy. We will be confiscating all large weapons from the mining camps and from New Kasbah. It may be there is a rebellion that needs to be quashed. We will see. But Caledonia will not be denied!"

He raised his fist in the air at the last sentence and the soldiers did the same, yelling in unison, "Caledonia will not be denied."

Kalju slid down the flyer with grace and began speaking with the officers, issuing instructions. Lt. General Matif stood at his side, looking concerned and crestfallen, all at the same time. Was he in on this treason?

By now the mechanics would have arrived in their cargo carriers at the camps, and be loading the large weapons.

Now he would see who was willing to stick their neck out and openly rebel.

CHAPTER 17 - CASSANDRA

CASSANDRA WOKE TO FIND XIXIA STIRRING. WAKING UP AND beginning to pack her things. Slowly everyone else got up and did the same.

Cassandra tore some etalia meat off what was left of one of the carcasses. She ate the rubbery, dried out strip of meat. Then washed it down with a sip of the last water she'd found.

They headed out quickly, in a hurry to get to their destination. They'd abandoned the wood from the stretcher a day ago, when Mia could walk an entire day. She'd been tired, but so pleased with herself. Samuel didn't have the heart to make her ride in the stretcher anymore.

They made good time during the very long day and most of them were surprised when they entered a long, narrow tunnel and Xixia began to run. Cassandra tried, but couldn't keep up. She let others pass her. Magda, Mia, Samuel and Cassandra walked along behind.

Up ahead there was much noise, most of it sounded joyful. They walked towards the light and entered into the most massive cavern she'd ever seen, with stalactites and stalagmites. There were three times as many homes as the last village. A stream cut through the center of the cavern, and stone bridges had been built over it.

There was a central flat area filled with Oachnik and a few humans. They joined them.

The cave had a musky scent to it and was lit with bluish tinted lights like she'd never seen before. They were distributed randomly on the ceiling and walls of the cave, casting an array of strange shadows because of the stalactites and stalagmites.

The four of them were crushed into the crowd and found themselves pushed into the middle of the circle. She'd never seen so many Oachnik. There were many, many youngsters, but also ones so elderly all their fur had grayed. A sort of lean fierceness defined them.

The crowd hushed to silence.

A group of elders sat in the center of the circle. When they finally came close to them, Xixia dropped to all fours. Cassandra did the same. Magda and Samuel followed.

"Please rise," said one of them, with a gravelly voice, speaking Earth Standard English, or ESE.

Cassandra was about a meter and a half from them. Xixia and Samuel stood. They had to help both Magda and Cassandra to their feet.

There were seven elders. Cassandra couldn't tell if they were male or female, but as her mother once said, *"If you can't tell, then it's none of your business, is it?"*

Oachnik didn't have the cultural divisions that humans sometimes had between men and women. Cassandra's reading had told her that the Caledonians were at the other extreme with very strict lines between genders. Maybe that was why they were such a warlike people.

"Welcome Xixia and our human guests. We are pleased to see you made it to Refuge, despite your difficulties."

Xixia bowed. Cassandra and the others did the same. Cassandra felt like she was standing in front of royalty. The Oachnik treated these elders with such respect.

She could smell the smoke of the cook fires and the meat roasting. Her stomach growled in response. They had walked long past their usual stopping time. How much meat did it take to supply this village? They must have vast herds of etalia. Or perhaps they didn't always eat meat.

Cassandra returned her gaze to the elders. Their eyes looked blank and she looked at Xixia. Hers did too. They must be speaking among themselves.

Magda wobbled next to her and Samuel grabbed her, supporting the older woman.

One of the elders gestured to a group of youngsters who quickly grabbed four wooden stools, formed from the curved branches of some bush. They set them behind Cassandra, Magda, Samule and Xixia. Cassandra gratefully sat down, as did Magda. Samuel remained standing, until Xixia sat on one. Then he looked so uncomfortable he finally sat down too.

One of the elders, the one with fur turned completely silver, returned to herself and stared at Cassandra.

"You were the one who thinks she saw the Gonsha?"

"Yes," Cassandra said.

"Show me," said the elder, gently entering her mind. Cassandra remembered the experience from waking till the time she glanced back and saw they were gone.

"You have never seen pictures of Gonsha, have you?"

"No. Just rumors of a dead race. And Xixia's description."

The elder gave a long, deep sigh.

"I have always suspected we didn't kill all of them. And for many years now, leaders have brought back information about signs they've seen that someone besides Oachnik are using the caves. We discounted it for a long time, saying it was just humans, exploring. I think we must admit to the possibility that the Gonsha still exist.

There were cries from the crowd. Cassandra could feel the wave of fear ripple all around her.

One of the other elders said, "So we must fight two wars. One with the Caledonians, the other with our old enemies, the Gonsha."

"It is possible," said the silver-furred elder, "but, it is also possible the Gonsha are very, very few and will not challenge us for a very, very long time. They have not harmed anyone."

"Let us hope so," said another elder.

"In the meantime," said the silver elder, "we should feed our guests. And let them rest. They have had weary work for many long marches. They need not concern themselves with our war."

Samuel said, "We would like to know how the war is going."

"Slowly," said a tall elder, with just a touch of white around his cheeks. "We are only able to halt their mining operations for a short time, before they make repairs and strengthen their security. They are mining in four different parts of the planet. Three are near water. We Oachnik live in those three places. We have left the other mining site untouched. We have petitioned the Governor, but he wouldn't listen and imprisoned our four messengers. They were tortured and killed. There will be no diplomatic solution to this problem. They are vermin who must be eliminated from our world."

Cassandra shuddered at the intensity of the words. Had one of them once said the same about the Gonsha? No, none of them could be that old. But some of their ancestors must have said the same thing. Would one of their descendants say the same about all humans?

"How will you accomplish such a thing?"

"Xixia told us of your plan to let the divine do its work on them. And to help them become … unbalanced. I think you humans should continue that work."

"None of us have been able to do that in days."

"You are tired," said the silver elder. "You need rest and to be outside with the sun, the wind and the moons. You are a people of the planet's surface, not the depths. We will take you outside tomorrow, when the sun is up. Now, eat. When you have finished we will show you your sleeping spaces. If you wish to bathe first, we will take you downstream. If you need anything else, please ask. We will speak again in the morning. It is time for us to sleep now."

She rose and the others followed. The crowd parted and many of the Oachnik left and went to separate houses. Obviously, they'd stayed up late, waiting for the last group to arrive.

A youngster brought Cassandra a plate of food and another a cup of liquid.

"Thank you," she said.

"Welcome," they said, shyly and skipped off to race around with a bunch of other young ones.

The four of them sat eating and were slowly joined by the rest of the group, who brought stools and sat down to eat. Some of the other villagers came over too. They spoke while Cassandra ate.

They'd arrived five and seven days ago. Not having run into the Caledonians, their treks had been faster. Out of about seventy-five villagers, only five had been lost. Shot by the Caledonians. That felt like sort of a miracle. In between bites, Marita and Samuel told them about their part of the adventure.

Marita told them about the reading Cassandra had done, card by card. They nodded solemnly, even those Cassandra knew had no belief in such things. Apparently, in her absence, they had decided that she was responsible for saving their lives. Cassandra had seen the warning of what the Caledonians would do and organized the exodus from the village. She was a hero.

That was much more responsibility than she really cared to take on.

CHAPTER 18 - KALJU

Kalju walked in a large circle outside the Council meeting room. The top of the butte was a lovely windswept place. Only his security detail was allowed up here, so it was relatively private. He could grow used to the view up here. Miles upon miles of rocky desert, each direction different than the previous.

The hot wind blasted his face, making him feel alive. While he waited for word of compliance by his Lt. Generals. There was no word yet from the mechanics collecting weapons from Lassorn or Ritgan.

Yutif had quickly complied with his order, no questions asked.

Matton had inquired whether he meant to deprive them of all their weapons, especially after they'd been attacked by the Oachnik, whom they'd repelled easily enough. Kalju restated his order, Matton acquiesced, and the maintenance crews got the weapons.

Kalju made another circle around the building, stretching his gait out. He was getting soft and needed to work out more than he had recently, but even just short walks left his knees aching. It was all those years spent fighting on Denna. The gravity there had been so strong it had destroyed many soldiers' bodies. Most had back problems.

His weak spot was clearly knees, which now ached at all times. Sometimes, it was worse and he took pain relievers. Which he hated. Having to take them made him feel weak.

The wind picked up intensity and brought with it clouds of sand from off the desert floor. Kalju went back inside and closed the door, brushing sand off his uniform.

He sat at the small table and looked at the tablet. Still no word from Lassorn or Ritgan. He rubbed his face, sand grit came away on his hands.

What would he do if they didn't respond?

They had to respond. Or put themselves at risk of a court martial. It was as simple as that.

Matif knocked on the door and brought in a fresh pitcher of rania.

"No more. I've had enough in the last day to rot my gut," said Kalju.

Matif nodded and began to leave.

"Lt. General, before you go, I wanted to tell you what happened at Camp #4." He proceeded to fill Matif in. As usual, the man's true thoughts were unreadable. The sign of a good officer, but damned hard to figure out.

"It's hard to believe that Lt. General Lassorn would do such a thing. He always had such a record for dependability."

"It could have been an accident. Unlikely though. We will have to wait and see if he hands over his weapons willingly."

Matif nodded. "Can I bring you anything else, Sir?"

"No thank you."

Matif left the room.

Kalju sent a report to Command, detailing his actions and listing the amounts of scillion which had shipped out already. Nearly all of it from Camp #3 from Lt. General Matton. Ritgan, at Camp #1, had finally got his equipment up and running and had begun pulling scillion out of the ground, when they were attacked by the natives. Their machinery was damaged and shut down.

Camp #2, Lt. General Yutif had just found scillion in the other half of the hill that his men were disassembling.

So far there was only silence from Lassorn.

He included in the message that it had been ten hours since he'd issued the commands and that Lt. Generals Lassorn and Ritgan had not yet complied. The maintenance crews hadn't reported in either.

Command hadn't messaged him about anything he'd sent them. That wasn't unusual. They had hundreds of planets to control. They also sat on information and watched how things developed before they acted. Contacting them was just another form of insurance for him. In case things turned ugly. Which it looked like it would soon.

Kalju poured a glass of water and held his wristband over the glass. It beeped a warning at him. The water contained a toxin. He looked at the analysis. The poison would kill him. Had Matif put it in there? Had he tested it?

He called two of his security men in from the hallway. Then messaged Matif that he needed him. Matif came up the elevator and entered the room. His expression looked almost annoyed.

"Lt. General, would you care to join me in a glass of water."

"No thank you, Sir. I'm not thirsty."

"That wasn't a question. It was an order."

Matif's expression changed to one of panic and he tried to run from the room. The heaviest security guard stopped him.

"So you did poison my water."

"I refuse to comment, Sir."

"Why?"

"I refuse to comment, Sir."

"You don't have the right to refuse."

Matif said nothing.

"Strip him of everything and put him in a cell down with the Council Members."

They hauled Matif off. The man struggled only a little.

How had he risen so high in rank?

Kalju accessed Matif's wristband information, but found nothing untoward. There were some messages sent to the other Lt. Generals, ones that Kalju had asked him to send. If there was treason there, it was encoded.

He sent yet another message to command, about Matif's attempt to poison him.

Then sat back in the chair.

He hadn't really expected this. Command *was* trying to kill him. In any way possible, it appeared. He wouldn't let the bastards win.

Question was, what was he going to do about it?

CHAPTER 19 - CASSANDRA

Cassandra slept for what felt like days. Trying to help her body recover from its trauma. She woke for a bit, ate and slept again. The younger folks healed faster than she did.

When Cassandra woke for good, it turned out she'd been down for two days.

She had slept in a small house, which was really only a room partitioned off from other rooms, inside the huge cavern. There was no ceiling. The room smelled like the freshly tilled soil that Cassandra experienced when she went to the date farm. The Oachnik slept on low beds made of wood and stuffed with brushgrass. Over that she'd put her sleepbag, but the Oachnik just slept on the dried, puffy grass. In retrospect, it was probably cleaner than her sleepbag.

Cassandra managed to sit up and sat there, groggily trying to remember where she was and how she'd gotten there.

There were voices outside the door, which was covered with sewn together etalia skins. They were speaking both her language and Oachnik. The sound was loud enough to hear, but quiet enough she couldn't catch the meaning of anything said.

Cassandra's mouth was dry and she needed to pee. Getting old was annoying. Her bones ached as she rose, especially the newly healed ankle. Cassandra didn't have to dress as she hadn't undressed when going to sleep.

What she wanted was to eat. Then go bathe, wherever the Oachnik bathed. Then wash all her clothes.

Then she might be ready to tackle understanding what had been happening with the Caledonians. Oh, and the Elders had said that they all needed to go be in the sunlight. She was ready for that, too.

She tried to smooth down her hair. Then pushed her way through the skins covering the short doorway.

Humans and Oachnik were sitting in small groups. Some were eating, others clustered around something on the ground. Another group were sparring, as if the Oachnik were teaching humans some of their fighting techniques. Which wasn't very practical for them since humans had no tails to balance themselves.

Every single being in the large cavern was busy doing something. An elder sat with a group of young ones, telling a story. The youngsters sat rapt, dark eyes glued to the elder, watching hand movements and facial expressions.

Marita came up to her and said, "Good morning."

"Hi, what's going on?"

"Everything. Come get some breakfast and I'll fill you in."

Cassandra followed her over to the fire where Marita handed her a clay bowl with rows of etalia painted on it. Marita scooped something tan with red streaks from a metal pot into it. The smell was amazing. Marita handed her a metal spoon and Cassandra dug in.

The sweet and tangy flavor of groundberries filled her mouth. Then a spice she couldn't name.

"What is this?"

"Groundberries with ground kiliya seed and some sort of spice I can't remember the name of. All cooked with etalia milk."

"It's wonderful."

"It is, isn't it? The Oachnik make the most fascinating food. Still, I think I'd kill for some soft goat cheese."

Cassandra ate while Marita explained what happened the last couple of days.

While she had been sleeping a rebellion had been growing. The Oachnik had taken all the humans who were awake, outside. To sit in the sun and feel the wind. People's abilities to use the powers given them by the divine had returned.

Each of them had chosen either a Caledonian or one of the villagers or Council Members held captive and were harassing them or boosting them up —depending on which side they were on. Marita had gotten to the Governor's Aide. Convinced him that the Governor saw him as a traitor and was going to have him tortured and killed. He'd bungled the attempted poisoning though, and was now imprisoned. Marita was searching for someone else to target next.

Magda had contacted her gold miner friend. Machinery had been damaged. Mining scillion wasn't going to happen at that site any time soon. Half of the Caledonians had been killed in the fighting. There were still enough left to guard the camp, just not as well as before.

They were in touch with other groups of Oachnik, who were working on the camps near them. Sabotaging them in any way possible. One group was slowly poisoning an entire camp, using an addictive herb in the mix so the Caledonians would keep eating the food.

Another band of Oachnik, one who'd lived close to humans for a long time, was using the Caledonians reaction to the divine, much like those traveling with Cassandra had. They were in contact with the man in charge of the camp and had worked on his fears, amplifying them to the point where he was mostly under their control.

"What should I do?" asked Cassandra.

"We need to get you outside and in the sunlight. Let your body heal and your powers return. Then you should do another reading. And decide," said Marita. "I could do with some sunshine."

"I need to bathe and wash all my clothes first, if that's

possible."

"I haven't washed mine yet. I'll come with you."

After cleaning up, Cassandra put on wet clothes, laid out the others to dry and followed Marita to the surface. There she found Mia and Samuel. Mia looked like the two days of rest had brought her closer to healing. Samuel looked much less weary than when Cassandra last saw him.

They sat close to a rock wall, blending in to the stone. They were in the blazing sun, but looked comfortable. Both of them had their eyes closed, so Cassandra didn't speak.

Marita and Cassandra sat near them on a massive boulder. Her wet clothes would dry in no time. She'd never been so glad to see the sun.

Cassandra had washed her long hair and left it loose. Now, she ran a brush and her fingers through it trying to untangle the knots. Once done with that, she separated it into three strands and began to braid it. The braid reached her waist. She thought about piling it all atop her head, but decided it would dry better down. All the water made it very heavy.

Marita had lain out flat on the boulder. Her eyes were closed as if asleep. But her breathing wasn't heavy. Was she trying to connect with someone?

Cassandra cleared her mind and tried to find Colin, Mazin, Aggripina or Alexander. Nothing.

Give yourself time.

She needed to recover first. Gather her strength. Reestablish a connection to the land.

So, she lay back on the rock. Felt the heat of the sun warm her. Dry the clothing on her body. Felt the warm breeze blow past, ruffling stray strands of hair. Smelled the dust, the earth around her. Even though she wasn't in her home anymore, this was home. This world, this planet. And she would fight to keep it safe and livable. Cassandra would do whatever she could to get the Caledonians off this planet.

As quickly as possible.

CHAPTER 20 - KALJU

KALJU STOOD INSIDE THE COUNCIL MEETING ROOM. CHECKING HIS tablet again for a response from Command. Nothing.

He strode to the window and looked out the vast desert of Titania. On the horizon a plume of sand rose up in a whirlpool of wind, spinning.

Straightening the black shirt of his uniform, he moved to another window. Farba had made no progress bringing in the escaped villagers and he'd lost men in the attempt.

Soldiers went into those cave systems searching for them and never returned. Lost men, lost equipment. Every one of those guns could now be in the hands of villagers and used against Caledonia. Finally, Farba had withdrawn and was sitting down in the village sulking.

Idiot. He should be sending flyers out, keeping the search going.

Kalju opened the door and went outside. The hot wind nearly bowled him over. He had to face into the wind, nearly bent over to stay upright. The soldier on this side of the building stood against the building. The man saluted.

"At ease," said Kalju.

His mouth felt dry. He could smell the ever-present sand scent on the wind. Not one of lush, well-watered soil, but the bitter smell of earth that rarely if ever felt water. Dust.

He coughed and went back inside where he could stand upright without as much effort. The door closed after him, the building trying to regulate temperature.

He had two choices. Either go along with Command and let one of the Lt. Generals kill him. Or to kill them first, maybe subdue them in some way. Was there a third choice? There must be. There always was.

A tiny voice spoke in his head, "You could disappear. Get off planet or go native. Find a quiet spot to relax and let go of all these nasty politics."

Where had that come from?

He'd never wanted a quiet place. But he *was* getting old. A bit too old for the rigors of soldiering. Even though he was in top physical condition, it wasn't what he'd been as a young man. He'd never regain that. His body would only decline. Which was why becoming a General had been a good thing. Until he got stuck here being Governor General.

He held his wristband over the glass of water sitting on the table. It pinged safe. He sipped the room temperature water, savoring the freshness of it. Rania had been making him feel bad lately. It upset his stomach. Water felt better.

So if he killed all the Lt. Generals, and it wasn't a test, but a coincidence they were conspiring against him, what would Command do? Have him executed, probably. Especially, if he couldn't prove it. And he didn't have anything damning yet.

So, the only options he could see right now were: death, murder at the risk of possible execution, or desertion with assured execution if he ever got caught.

Not a good choice among them.

He *could* stage his own death, and desert.

A message pinged in. He checked the tablet. Ritgan's large artillery had been picked up. Lassorn's hadn't. Apparently, it had been stolen. At least that's what maintenance staff had been told. They were on their way back to New Kasbah.

So, Lassorn wasn't willing to openly rebel. Ritgan may or may not be a party to this.

Kalju composed a message and sent it to Command about the missing equipment, which he suspected Lassorn had tucked away somewhere.

Before he could finish it, another message pinged in. It was air control.

"Sir, we're getting an emergency alert signal from the maintenance ship. They've had to land and have been boarded. Natives have taken them prisoner. We don't know if they're alive. Someone turned the signal off and there's no response to our requests."

Damn. Lassorn or Ritgan must be behind this.

"Where did they land?"

"Quadrant 25 sir."

He looked at the map. It was just beyond Naritana and Camp #4. Lassorn must be responsible.

"Send a couple flyers out and see what you can find. Tell them to take care, the rebels are fully armed with our weapons."

"Will do, Sir."

Kalju straightened up and walked over to the window.

So, Lassorn wanted to cast this as the natives rebelling, did he?

He messaged the Colonels who were here at New Kasbah. Instructed them to use the weapons taken from Mattorn, Yutif and Farba and arm all the flyers possible.

Kalju wished there were still some natives nearby. They'd all fled with the villagers. Every, single one. He could use some information. To see if they were really a threat, or if it had been Lassorns' men masquerading as natives that had taken the ship, and the men.

He needed a strategy. Lassorn wasn't going to sit around waiting for him to act. The man had a plan and he was willing to use it.

Kalju sat and looked at the cargo manifests of the ships which picked up the scillion and delivered it to the massive father ship orbiting the planet. Scillion was piling up in the father ship, although not fast enough.

He paced around the edges of the octagonal room. As he walked, anger built inside him. Anger at Lassorn, but mostly anger at Command.

They were hanging him out to dry. Sending five Lt. Generals after him. Some had been sent because they were completely incompetent. For others, it was clearly a test. To prove they were worthy of higher command.

He'd been commanded to do the same when he was younger and lower in rank. Survival of the fittest.

But he was finished playing that game. He'd clearly made it as high in rank as they would let him go.

A plan began to form in his head, a very good plan.

He took the elevator down to where the prisoners were housed.

CHAPTER 21 - CASSANDRA

Cassandra helped the others prepare food for the Oachnik who were readying an attack on one of the mining camps. She cut strips of etalia meat with a very large knife. Then laid them out on a rock near the fire, salted them and left them to cook and dry out.

Her ankle had healed fully and she could walk back and forth without limping now. She went back to the carcass and cut more strips of meat. Every single part of the etalia were used by the Oachnik. Skins were tanned and used for door coverings. Some of the humans were using them for blankets. The horns, hooves and bones were carved into beads and dyed with various plant leaves, flowers and roots. Many of the organs were cooked in an intense stew-like concoction that, with enough spices added, even Cassandra had to admit was tasty.

Being out in daylight helped her gifts return. She had felt unnatural without them.

She was able to get in contact with Aggripina, Mazin and Colin. They didn't have much to report, but were trying to help keep the Caledonian soldiers unstable.

She was also in touch with several of the villagers who'd stayed and were now prisoners. Alexander was recovering, with the help of Thomas, the village doctor. Their guards were unhappy. They'd been grumbling about the Governor. He'd been giving very peculiar orders that they didn't understand. And he spent a great deal of time talking to himself as he walked to and fro. There wasn't a soldier who couldn't wait to get off the planet.

Cassandra asked Xixia if she was able to get into the Governor's mind and the Oachnik just smiled at her with a wide smile and those sharp, pointy teeth.

Cassandra took that for a yes.

Later that day, the elders gathered and the silver-furred elder said, "Xixia tells us that you are an oracle. Our people used to be able to hear what our world wanted from us. We lost that gift when we murdered all the Gonsha. That was a mistake, even though to this day we do not know what we could have done differently. The Gonsha were determined to exterminate every single one of us. Would you do us the honor of looking into the future? Of giving us advice?"

"I would be honored to do so," Cassandra said.

She went to her pack and got her cards and a scarf.

Then sat down in front of the elders, spreading the scarf on the stone in front of her. She took the cards out and asked, "What are your questions?"

The silver-furred elder asked, "Are the Gonsha alive and what should we do about them?"

The tall elder with white cheeks spoke next, "How shall we rid our planet of the Caledonians?"

The smallest elder who had white rings around her eyes asked, "How should we repair the damage they've done?"

Cassandra shuffled the cards, keeping their questions in mind.

"The first card is the Hermit. This is about shutting out distractions in order to get one's spiritual or other work done. Focus on working towards perfection, by eating well, resting and moving closer to your goals. Seek material security and self-sufficiency so that you can retreat and live in union with the sacred and eternal. Use the power and knowledge you gain to create, heal and guide others."

The silver-furred elder nodded and said, "The Gonsha are a distraction right now. Perhaps by retreating, we shall learn how to meet with them when it is time."

Cassandra said, "The second card is the Man of Crystals, the inventor. You invent new ideas. Experience a creative explosion of the mind, and use your ideas. Revolutionize your world. Play with ideas, spin them around and look at them from different angles."

The tall elder nodded and said nothing.

"The third card is the Child of Crystals, the learner. Learn by exploring new ideas. Examine your belief and break through the fear of letting go of old beliefs which have kept you safe in the past. Learn new values which bring you growth and expansion. See the world as a child does—full of wonder and magic."

"So we must search for new ways to repair the damage they've done," said the smallest elder.

"The last card is the key card, which ties everything together. It is the Ten of Cups, passion. You are excited and alive with energy. Don't be afraid to show your feelings. Be self confident and powerful. Show your passion. I think it is important to show yourselves to the Caledonians."

"It is true," said Xixia. "My travels into the Governor's mind says they have underestimated us. They think we are weak."

"Then we shall surprise them," said the silver-furred elder. "We will most certainly surprise them."

Cassandra asked, "What can I do to help?"

"You already have, young one. We may ask you for direction again. Your people are not warriors. We must keep you safe, while we make war. You can help teach our children that we share this world with those who would not destroy it. Those who threaten us, we will destroy. And perhaps someday, we will be ready to communicate that to the Gonsha. We wish to live in peace with all beings. Those that cannot abide harmony are not welcome on this world."

The silver-furred elder stood and bowed to everyone and walked off towards one of the small caves, her tail held high.

The other elders left soon after, talking Oachnik between themselves. Making plans. Cassandra could understand bits of their conversation, but not enough to make sense of it.

The Oachnik were going to make war on the Caledonians. Who were highly armed. Although Xixia had said something about the big guns being taken away from three of the mining camps as a result of the Governor's increasing paranoia.

Still, it would be guns against what?

She'd never seen the Oachnik fight. Had never seen them with weapons. Although she knew they used human guns when they needed them. With all the soldiers they'd gotten lost in the caves, the Oachnik had probably amassed quite a collection of weaponry. But the Caledonians had more.

Had she led them into this? She didn't want to be responsible for their deaths.

CHAPTER 22 - KALJU

Kalju walked down the long white hallway past the prison cells. It smelled of unwashed bodies despite the air circulation system. It was time to turn these people loose. Although that would put them at the mercy of Farba and his men. Where could he put Farba so the man could cause no trouble?

The back of his mind continued to work on the maze, trying to find him a way out of this mess. There had to be one.

He stopped in front of the cell containing the former Councilor. The man's bruises were healing and he looked alert, pacing around the cell.

Kalju signaled the guard to let him in.

Colin looked over, his face filled with panic. Then it shifted slightly, the fear dying back to wariness.

"Are they treating you better?" asked Kalju.

"Yes, thank you."

"Good. The other villagers are being looked after as well. My Lt. General has no understanding of politics. I have reassigned him."

"Are all of them okay? What about Aggripina and Mazin?" asked Colin.

"All healthy as far as I know. A couple of the villagers were ill and we made sure they got medication that the doctor who's imprisoned with them said was needed. They are better now."

So, which of the other villagers was the man so concerned about? That might provide some leverage if he needed it.

Colin nodded.

"What do you know about the natives of this planet?"

The Councilor's eyebrows rose in surprise. "They're deeply connected with the land. Kind and compassionate, if you're their friend. If you're not, they are formidable enemies."

"Did they work with the Council?"

"Of course. We took took the Oachnik into our confidence. Asked their opinion on things which affected them. Asked their help for information about the planet. They were a part of our community."

"You say were?"

"Did you capture any of them with the villagers or other Council Members?"

"No."

"They've vanished, haven't they? Gone back to their own villages. To safety."

"The only sign of them has been attacks on the mining operations."

"If they're attacking them, there's a reason. Could be the mining is threatening the ground stability in those areas. The Oachnik live in caverns deep beneath the surface. You may be damaging villages you didn't even know existed. Or threatening a water supply."

Kalju nodded.

"How can I get word to them that I'd like to talk to them?"

"Some of the more nomadic groups used to pass through New Kasbah from time to time. They traded with the merchants. I don't know if any of the villagers might know. The Council simply told the Oachnik who came to meetings or those who lived in the village, and word would get back to the elders rather quickly if it was a matter of importance."

"So the Oachnik lived with humans. Did humans ever live with the Oachnik?"

"Some have. There was an anthropologist who came to Titania 37. She stayed with them for several years, traveling between the villages. Then went back to her home planet to collect all her documentation. Most humans don't want to live underground."

Kalju could understand that. He liked the feeling of the wind on his face.

He got up and said, "Thank you, you've been very helpful."

"Might I ask if I could see the villagers?"

"I will consider it," said Kalju.

The guard let him out and he walked out of the Council building to the prisoners' new quarters. The blue-colored portable housing was made of a new plastic. Cheap, sturdy and easy to construct. It was not well ventilated and felt hot inside.

Many of the prisoners were sleeping. Others sat on two plastic bunks, talking. They stopped when he stood in front of their door, and looked at him through the clear panel.

"Let me in," said Kalju.

"Sir, it's not safe."

"They're unarmed, some of them are crippled. What are they going to do?"

"Sir, we're outnumbered. It goes against protocol."

"Well, then get some more guards down here."

The guard radioed for more guards and an elevator brought half a dozen guards, on full alert.

"I'm going in alone. You can wait out here. If there's trouble, storm in and attack. I don't expect any trouble."

"Sir, we must go in with you. Regulations," said the guard.

"All right, two of you can come in and stand by this wall. In an unthreatening manner, weapons away."

The guard in charge nodded.

By the time Kalju came inside, all of the prisoners stood clustered together. The guards did as he asked, but they couldn't seem to manage the unthreatening part.

Kalju spoke to the prisoners, "My apologies for disturbing you. I trust that you're being treated better than before."

"Yes," said the doctor. "Thank you for the medicine."

"I'm not going to waste your time. I would like to speak with some of the natives. The Oachnik. Do you know how I can reach them?"

Silence.

"It's important. The sooner we finish our mission here, the sooner you can get back to your village and your lives."

"You're really going to release us?" asked a burly man with red hair.

"Yes. I am. There's no sense in killing you. That's just wasteful."

"But the officer who beat us… ."

"Has been reassigned. I don't like to speak ill of my soldiers, but he is an incompetent bully who I'm stuck with. It happens sometimes."

"Then let us go now," said an elderly woman.

"I cannot. He is guarding the village. It wouldn't be safe for any of you to get in his way."

The man who had mechanical legs spoke, "I can get hold of them. I have a radio in my meat shop."

"They use radios?"

"Yeah. Old tech, but it works."

"Take me there, I'd like you to send a message for me."

The man looked surprised, but said, "I can do that. Sometimes it takes days for them to answer."

"We'll make it work," said Kalju. "Follow me."

The man glanced back at his companions.

"I will bring you back, after you've sent the message."

The man followed him, moving slowly. Kalju slowed his pace so the man could keep up.

"What's your name?"

"Angel."

"You speak the Oachnik's language?"

"Yes.

They walked out of the portable, followed by the soldiers. The area around the Council Complex was abuzz with soldiers going about their daily business.

Kalju cut through them and signaled for all but two of the soldiers who'd been called to follow. He led them towards the small flyer that was at his disposal.

Why hadn't the Council built a transport system between here and New Kasbah? He decided they must have wanted the separation from the village. The Council Complex was larger than the village and seemed self-contained.

It turned out that Angel was one of the local meat vendors. His shop was one of those that lined the market square, now deserted except for some of Farba's soldiers.

The shop had a windowed front. Angel pressed his palm on the door and it slid open. The place smelled surprisingly clean, although a chemical clean, like chlorine. It looked sterile, all the surfaces silver and white. No food left out, despite the sudden appropriation of the village.

Angel led them to a back room, an office. The walls lined with fake blonde wood and a faux wood desk. An ancient radio sat on a cabinet. It was turned off. Angel switched it on.

"What message do you want to send?"

"I would like one of them to come to the Council Complex so I can speak with them. Without an interpreter. I want one of them who can understand our language."

Angel spoke into the microphone in a language that was rolling and guttural and had clicking sounds. Then he sent it in the common language. When he finished, the man said, "The message has gone out. I should sent it two or three more times, an hour or two between, just to make sure it gets heard."

"Let's unplug this and take it back to the Council Complex."

"That might work," said Angel. "There's an antennae up on the roof."

Two soldiers carried it out to the flyer. Angel locked his shop, after looking around longingly. What must it be like to have a stable life, on one planet? In one village? What did one's world look like when it was that small?

Back at the Complex, Kalju had them take the radio up to the Council Chambers. Angel made sure it worked, then sent another message.

"It may be that they don't send a return message. They might just send someone here," said Angel.

He showed Kalju how to send and receive a message and coached him how to say, "Please wait while I get someone who speaks Oachnik."

Kalju had always struggled with foreign languages. They didn't come easily to him or make much sense. And no one had been able to create a mechanical translator that worked well enough for diplomacy.

The guard took Angel back to the other prisoners. They brought him back every two hours until four messages had been sent out. No reply came back. Kalju paced restlessly around the Council Chamber.

Perhaps the Oachnik weren't the way out for him.

CHAPTER 23 - CASSANDRA

CASSANDRA HELPED PREPARE WHAT THE OACHNIK CALLED TRAVELING food. Dried etalia and gwandyuck meat chopped into bits and mashed with dried wassia berries and dried dates. These were rolled into about 2 1/2 centimeter-sized balls.

She rolled the balls with forty other humans and Oachnik. Humans who, like her, weren't much good for anything else.

The warriors, human and Oachnik were training and packing to move. Their attack on another one of the scillion mining camps was imminent.

Cassandra sat on a hard stone boulder, scooped another handful of meat and fruit and rolled them together. There was enough fat on the gwandyuck to melt and keep the balls stuck together as it solidified again. The fat left a greasy residue on her hands. It was meditative work which allowed her mind to wander.

She contacted Colin.

"I am safe," he said. *"The Governor seems to just want to get the scillion and get off Titania."*

She contacted Alexander and he told her, *"The Governor told us that he intends to let us return to our village."*

"Do you believe him?"

"Yes. Although I overheard the guards saying that the man is going crazy."

"The divine?"

"They didn't elaborate, but that was our thinking. All of us villagers are still together."

She shifted on the boulder, her muscles ached from the cold stone. She should go sit out in the sun for a while. Maybe after she emptied this bowl of food.

Xixia sat nearby doing the same work at twice the speed.

"Have you been working on the Governor?"

Xixia grinned, showing her first row of teeth.

"Yes, he is ripening quite nicely."

"When will he be ready to pick?"

"Soon. Have patience. We will pick him soon."

Cassandra sighed. She wished to be back in her shop, going about her day to day business. Reading cards or runes, helping people sort out their lives. Not going to war.

A group of three young Oachnik, machine guns strapped over one shoulder and across their bodies, raced into the cavern. Everyone looked up from their work. They ran towards a walled enclosure where Cassandra knew the elders often spent time talking about what needed to be done.

Several Oachnik left their work and stood, including Xixia.

"Messengers," Xixia said to Cassandra.

Cassandra wiped her hands on a coarse rag woven from dried grass stems. Then followed Xixia into the gathering crowd. Someone in front said something in Oachnik, Cassandra caught part of it.

"Message from New Kasbah."

Mostly, everyone stood silently, waiting. Finally the tall elder with white fur on his cheeks came out of the doorway that was covered with etalia hides and looked around.

"It is a message from the Governor. He would like to speak with one of us. We will consider this message. That is all, go back to your work."

Then he went back inside, the hides on the door covering the room again.

The three young Oachnik went to the cooking area and took food and water. They were surrounded by those wanting to know more.

"That is all there is," said one of them.

"Nothing more?"

"Nothing more."

"It is a trap."

"It must be."

"Perhaps he has heard of our growing army and wishes to make a truce."

The debate continued around the three young ones, who just listened, occasionally nodding or shrugging, but mostly eating. As if they hadn't eaten in days.

Xixia stood by the doorway, waiting.

"There is nothing more, but at least it is something."

"Do you think it's a trap?" asked Cassandra

"Who can say? It might be, might not. The man is becoming desperate. He's looking for a way out of his life."

"He could always just pack up and leave the planet."

Xixia shook her head. "His people would hunt him down and kill him. No, he needs a clever way out."

"Will you give him one?"

"It is not mine to give. It is the elders who decide his fate."

The meeting inside must be very important. Cassandra didn't understand why, but all her instincts told her so. She closed her eyes and went deep inside, waiting as patiently as she could.

A small voice inside her said, *"This is your work. You must do this, you must go."*

Not long after a voice inside said, "Xixia and Cassandra, you may enter."

Xixia went in and Cassandra followed her.

The elders sat on their haunches on woven mats spread in a circle. They moved aside slightly, leaving two places open.

"Please sit and talk with us," said the silver-furred elder.

The white-cheeked elder asked, "What have you to tell us about this man Xixia?"

"I have been working on him. Assisting the divine. He resists the divine, which makes him afraid of everything and everyone around him. He believes everyone is out to ruin him. He is moving towards insanity."

"Is he a danger for us to meet with him?" asked the silver elder.

"I do not believe so. I think he's looking for a way out. He wants to escape from his work. He believes his men are trying to kill him. I also believe some of them are. Being on our planet is a test for all of them. To see who will win. It is the way his people choose leaders. He would like to quit. His danger is his instability."

"Will you and Cassandra go meet with him?"

"What would you like us to say?"

"We would offer him refuge if that is what he seeks. Provided his people leave our planet. They are poisoning the water," said an elder with pink skin showing in her large ears.

"We will go," said Xixia.

Cassandra didn't even have a chance to say yes.

"We can leave as soon as we are prepared," said Xixia

"We will send five young ones to accompany you. You will need to travel quickly."

"We can do that."

Xixia rose and Cassandra followed her, they bowed to the elders and left.

"Pack only what you need, travel light. We will each need to carry our own food. Luckily there is a lot of traveling food for us to bring."

"Luckily, I'm in better shape than I was when I left New Kasbah," said Cassandra.

She walked to the tiny room where her belongings lay. Stuffed her sleepsack and a spare set of clothes in her pack, leaving behind many of the things she'd brought. Her tarot cards would need to come along though. And her walking stick.

She picked up the pack and went out to fill a water bottle and get traveling food.

Marita came up beside her and asked, "Where are you going?"

"To the Council Complex."

"Didn't we just come from New Kasbah?"

"There is a need," said Xixia, coming up to fill Cassandra pack food.

It took them all of half an hour to get ready to leave. The elders came out to say goodbye. Then they and five younglings were off. They set off into a deep cave.

"This one runs straight towards New Kasbah for a very long while," said Xixia.

They walked and Cassandra felt very strong. They moved at a rapid pace for at least half a day. Not even stopping to eat. They just pulled the traveling food from their packs and kept walking. Cassandra had to admit it tasted good. Salt, meat and berries, she wouldn't have thought it would. Tart wassia berries, sweet dates and salted, rich meat. Chewing it took some time. Then she'd sip water.

They kept going until finally Cassandra said, "I need to rest."

They walked until they came to a cavern and sat on some rocks for probably half an hour.

"Can you go farther today or do you need to sleep?" asked one of the youngsters.

"I can go on. How many days at this pace?"

"It will take us four days to get to New Kasbah," said the youngster.

Four days of walking. Well, that was much less than the way here. They had split up and gone to the Oachnik base the long way on the first trip. Probably had been afraid the Caledonians would follow the large mass of humans from New Kasbah. Hopefully the Caledonians hadn't found this way in on their own and there would be no trouble.

Was the Governor already insane or just on his way? Would they be able to get the Caledonians off the planet? Cassandra mulled all this over, turned the problem around in her mind as they walked through the tunnel. This one was quite large and clear of debris. It was obviously well used.

It curved occasionally, but mostly led them in a straight line. She used a dim light to see by. The Oachnik of course needed none. This was their natural element. Although their eyes seemed to adapt well to sunlight, too.

She kept going, trudging along. At the end of the day, she fell into her sleep sack and slept until the next morning.

The next three days were the same.

The morning of the fourth day was something else entirely.

CHAPTER 24 - KALJU

KALJU PACED AROUND THE COUNCIL CHAMBER AGAIN. ALL THE doors were open and the wind blasted hot. Sand coated everything in the room. Kalju's rage shimmered in the wind.

All the heavy artillery except Lassorn's had been picked up and brought to the Complex. Ritgan had finally surrendered his, after much argument. The fact that he would even argue with such an order was absurd. In response, Kalju would need to punish him.

Besides reporting him to Command, he'd need to come up with an effective punishment. Cutting ration deliveries to the camp would merely deprive the men, not the Lt. General.

He'd have to find something else.

Now that he had nearly all the weapons, he could attack Lassorn's camp. Although the man would be ready for such an attack. Lassorn had probably planned everything before he even came on planet. So Kalju was merely reacting. He needed to outsmart the bastard. But how?

The natives were the key in all this. He needed to speak with them. See if they would take him in. Keep him hidden from Caledonia. Then make Command's entire plan explode.

That would be difficult. He'd set events in motion already. Things he couldn't stop. The Lt. Generals were either pissed off by his taking their large weapons away or completely oblivious and incompetent. No man with any pride would deal with having their weapons removed. It just wasn't done. But he had and they were angry. Rightly so.

It had been an extreme measure to keep air transport safe. Their mission was to mine scillion as fast as possible, not fight a war amongst themselves.

But Lassorn had made the first move. He'd screwed everything up. Now war was at hand.

And Kalju would eliminate every single one of the bastards, guilty of treason or not, because he could no longer tell the difference.

He should have been able to pick his own Lt. Generals for this mission. He only slid by with being able to pick his own security.

He'd sent Farba back into the desert, on foot, with only a handful of men to continue hunting for the villagers. Then reassigned the rest of Farba's men to guarding the Council Complex, and the villagers held prisoner within. He wasn't a hundred percent sure where their loyalties lay.

Most of his own men were gearing up for an attack on Lassorn's camp. Unless Kalju changed his mind at the last minute. Perhaps he should attack the other camps first. Get all their small weapons, eliminate any hindrances. Or use his full power on Lassorn. There were good and bad points with each plan.

A message pinged in on his tablet and he ceased pacing. He drank from his water glass and read the message.

Farba. His men were deep in one of the caves and ran into a sentient native that wasn't Oachnik. They'd taken it prisoner, but not before it attacked them and killed two men. It was fierce and terrifying.

There were no other sentient natives on Titania. Only the Oachnik. It must be an alien, landed and living in the caves. Interesting.

He ran his fingers through his longish hair. He hadn't cut it since arriving on the planet. He'd have to grow it out if he wanted to pass for an immigrant. One who'd come in on one of the supply ships that brought goods to Titania 37. He didn't want anyone to figure out he was a Caledonian and give him away. Until he made a final decision, it would just have to stay.

Kalju looked down. His hands were shaking. He couldn't even control his body anymore. There was so much riding on this decision, the rest of his life for one thing. If he did this, he was throwing his life as a Caledonian away. The life he'd worked at for twenty-five years. His entire career.

But then Command hadn't exactly given him a choice.

He paced around the room, ticking off the wrongs they'd done to him on his fingers. Breathing in the smell of dry sand.

No, he'd just do it. Begin the war. Destroy as much of Lassorn as he could. Make the man pay for being a part of ruining his life.

He pushed a button on his tablet.

"Captain Naton, it's a go. Repeat, it's a go."

"Understood Governor General. In progress."

Kalju sank into the chair and drooped, his head and shoulders over onto the table. Weeping like a woman as he heard the newly armed flyers roar off into the sky.

CHAPTER 25 - CASSANDRA

Cassandra woke to the sound of the Oachnik rising. She got out of her sleepsack quickly, rolled it up, stuffed it into her pack and pulled out water and food.

Within minutes they were off again.

They had walked all morning when the younglings and Xixia ahead of her stopped completely in the middle of a tunnel.

Ahead was a large cavern with noise coming from it. Talking.

And it wasn't in Oachnik.

Cassandra didn't recognize the language, but she didn't know that many. Probably some off-worlders mucking about in the caves. The Caledonians had probably driven many beings underground. She moved forward slightly, trying to see and hear better.

The noise sounded like wailing and then hushed speaking. As if someone was trying to comfort someone else. Or perhaps several someones.

She couldn't see.

Xixia and the younglings blocked the tunnel. Xixia stood paralyzed, stiff against the cave wall. The younglings as well.

Finally, Cassandra pushed through them and slowly walked forward.

What she saw were five Gonsha clustered together. Two of them bent over double, sitting on a large boulder in the cavern, moving forward and back, wailing. The other three hunched around the two, patting and hugging them and making the crooning noises.

What had happened? It sounded terrible.

Cassandra turned to the Oachnik and looked at Xixia questioningly. Xixia returned her gaze, but the Oachnik's fear was palpable.

It was an old fear. From the time when the Gonsha and Oachnik had been at war. Before the Oachnik did their best to exterminate the Gonsha. Did the hatred still exist between them?

Cassandra had to do something. She walked out into the cavern, cleared her throat and stood near the tunnel entrance.

The seated Gonsha leapt to their feet.

"Oh hello, is everything all right?" she asked in the common language.

They stared at her. Ready to flee. Not fight, she noticed.

"I mean you no harm. I'm simply concerned."

One of them spoke to the others, a grumbling noise. They were tall, perhaps eight feet tall. Their fur looked bluish-white in Cassandra's dim light. Like ghosts. Their long, ropy tails flipped around nervously. They wore leather belts from which hung jeweled scabbards with long, curved swords. Two of them carried machine guns like the Caledonians used. Their hands which looked like they had too many long fingers, ended in sharp, curved claws.

Finally, one of them replied in the common tongue, "The invaders. They took one of our young ones."

"Which invaders?" Cassandra asked.

"The ones who wear fur the color of darkness."

Fur the color of darkness? What did that mean? The color of darkness. Black. The Caledonians?

"Do you mean clothes? Clothes the color of darkness?" she asked, tugging on her baggy shirt.

"Yes, clothes. We did not know the name of your fur was different," said the Gonsha, mouthing the word clothes. "We killed several and took their weapons. They killed three of us. We are not many. Not like in our ancestors' time."

"When did this happen?" Cassandra asked.

"In the time it has taken to run from them."

"Not long, then?"

"Not long."

Their eyes widened and Cassandra noticed Xixia and the younglings had come up behind her.

"None of us is going to hurt the others, do you understand me?" Cassandra asked, looking at both groups.

Xixia nodded, and the young ones lowered their weapons.

"This planet is large enough for all of us to share peaceably. Perhaps not with the Caledonians though, they want to destroy it. We are going to meet with them. We will try to get your young one back," Cassandra told the Gonsha.

"Why would you do such a thing?"

"It is the right thing to do. And we can. Their leader wants something from us. We have the means to give it to him. We will make him pay for it."

One of the Gonsha who'd been wailing stepped forward and said, "I will come with you. I carried my child in my body, gave birth to him. I will come and get him back."

"I will come too. I am his family," said the other wailing Gonsha.

The remaining Gonsha looked at each other and then stepped forward.

"We will all come, if we may."

"They won't let you come meet with them if you're carrying weapons," Cassandra said, to both the Oachnik who were armed, and the Gonsha. "It's the way they are. Always afraid."

"We will leave our weapons in the desert," the Gonsha said.

"So will we," said one of the Oachnik.

With that they were off. The Oachnik younglings led the way. Cassandra followed them. The Gonsha came at the end.

Cassandra noticed when everyone stopped for her to rest that the younglings moved a little closer to the Gonsha and they admired each others' weapons.

It was a long march that day. When they finally left the caves, it was night outside. Just past the middle of the night according to the goat stars. Cassandra basked in the feel of the dry wind on her face. The smells of sand and sweet brushgrass filled her nose.

Cassandra was a different woman than when she'd left here, a few weeks ago. Harder and stronger. More sure of herself, even though she'd always been sure of herself.

The Caledonians would be on alert. Nervous at night. Or perhaps not. Perhaps they'd grown lax with no challenges to face.

By the time they'd gotten to New Kasbah, dawn was breaking. The villages was completely deserted. No soldiers. Just a couple of brazen rats who looked up at them curiously.

They continued on up the road to the Council Complex, all of them unarmed, having cached their weapons among the rocks. She still had her walking stick, although that wasn't a weapon. The Gonsha and Oachnik had fearsome claws and teeth.

At the entrance to the Complex stood a soldier. Cassandra went first, and said, "Governor Kepa is expecting us."

The man looked at them wide-eyed and said, "What?"

"Young man, listen up. I said Governor Kepa is expecting us. He sent a message. We have traveled a long way to get here."

"He's probably sleeping."

"He won't thank you if we leave," Cassandra said. "I am an old woman and I can't stand here all night. I need food and water and a place to sit down. I'd guess some of the Oachnik and Gonsha here feel the same. We've been traveling for days. Walking. Now you'd better get a message to the Governor or your head will probably leave your body. He said it was urgent."

The man spoke into his wristband and listened to the response.

"Just a minute," he said.

He listened to another message on his wristband while Cassandra took deep breaths.

"I'm to take your weapons and let you in," he said, a puzzled look on his face.

"We have no weapons," Cassandra said.

He looked them over, walking around each being and then spoke into the wristband. The doors to the lobby of the Council Complex opened.

It was light and airy in the lobby. Cool air with fountains running everywhere. The Gonsha and Oachnik looked around in wonder. Except Xixia. She'd probably been there before. As a go-between for the Council and Oachnik elders.

Cassandra had never been there before. Had no reason to. She marveled at the expensive glass and the moisture in the air. The room smelled wonderful, green and earthy.

A soldier came up to meet them and said, "Governor General Kepa will meet you in the Council Chambers. If you'll follow me, please."

They followed him to an elevator. When the door closed and it began to move, the Gonsha grumbled.

Cassandra held her hands out at waist level, closed her eyes and made a motion that everyone should calm down. It seemed to work. Either that or they were busy trying to figure out what it meant.

The elevator stopped and they got out in a small entryway. The doors in front of them were open. Just outside of the elevator doors stood two heavily armed soldiers. The soldiers looked at them with narrowed eyes.

Cassandra walked into the large room, bare except for two small tables. One heavily laden with electronic equipment. Old electronic equipment. The other had a small tablet on it.

At the far end of the room by the open full-length windows stood a disheveled man in uniform. He looked barely recognizable from the vids she'd seen when the Caledonians first arrived. His hair, several inches long and not brushed. His face, unshaven for many days. Even his uniform looked rumpled. His eyes were bloodshot and his face had a strained look.

"Cassandra," she said and held out my hand.

He shook it, a peculiar look on his face, "I'm Governor Kalju Kepa. Do you have a last name?"

"Never use it," she said, sitting in the only chair.

CHAPTER 26 - KALJU

The woman was being disrespectful. Sitting in his chair, uninvited. Then again, she was a civilian. And old. Maybe she didn't know. Or perhaps it was intentional and she intended to control this meeting. Either way, he wasn't going to acknowledge it.

She said, "You called us here?"

All the Oachnik stood behind her, letting her do the speaking. The other beings too. He had no idea what they were. The one Farba had brought back had said nothing. It seemed catatonic when spoken to, but attacked viciously when not restrained. Their size felt intimidating.

Finally, Kalju spoke.

"Yes, I called you here, but I don't know who all of you are. I've never seen the like of these fellows." He nodded to the blueish white furred aliens.

"They are Gonsha. Natives of this planet. You have taken one of them and they are very upset and angry. You have kidnapped their child. I don't think any one of us wants to see them get angrier."

"I won't waste your time. I have a problem," Kalju said.

He'd rehearsed the speech to himself several times. And

needed to get it just right, but wasn't sure what would appeal to such a diverse group. Kalju hated talking to women. They were emotional and incomprehensible. Old women were even worse than young ones. They were conniving.

"I have been given several Lt. Generals to work for me. Some of them are good competent men. Some of them are not. And some of them are out to kill me. My superiors see this as a game, I believe. A test, to see who will win. I don't want to play anymore."

"Go on," said the woman.

She was obviously used to taking charge. It annoyed him.

"I want out of this mess. I need your help. I need to disappear from Caledonia's view. Permanently."

"What would happen to your men? All the other Caledonians? They are poisoning what precious little water exists on our planet."

"I have a plan. To get them off planet. I need your help."

His mind was reeling. Filled with worry about the Lt. Generals and their plots to kill him. The complexity of his plan, of everything going right.

"I don't see what kind of help we can be," said the woman.

"I need the Oachnik, and I guess, the Gonsha, to attack several of the mining camps at once. I will command my soldiers to retreat to the supply ship orbiting above. You will need to deal with anyone left behind."

"How will that help you escape from your superiors?"

"I will arrange to have my shuttle to appear to crash where it will never be found. With me on it."

"Where will you go?" asked the woman.

"I don't know. I can't leave the planet, they'll be able to track my ship. I was hoping to be taken in by the Oachnik, until I can leave with one of the usual supply ships that come to your planet."

The woman was silent, but her expression told him that she was shocked. He said nothing. Just waited.

"Do you have any idea how the Oachnik live?"

"Not much. I know they live in mostly underground, in the caves."

"They live very, very simply. And communally."

"I have always lived with others. That's what soldiers do. And we live simply."

"You would be allowed no weapons."

"I am finished fighting. I have lost my stomach for it." Was that true? Had he really? Kalju's soldiering years had been the best of his life. "I am finished fighting like I am now. It's all politics. I don't want to live like this anymore."

"Risen above your competence level?" she asked, insultingly.

He wanted to punch her, but resisted the urge. Because she was right.

"Yes, I have. I'm no good at politics. I don't understand the complexities."

They were all silent, staring at him. Kalju felt a great energy among them. As if they were talking silently among themselves. Could Oachnik, Gonsha, and even humans do that?

"Please," he said.

"You must release the Gonsha you've taken prisoner first. Before we will even consider your request."

"Done," he said, punching the request into the tablet. "The child will be brought here. The Lt. General who took him is one of my problems. The man is a fool."

"What are the locations of the mining camps?" asked the woman.

Kalju pulled up a map on the tablet and showed them. Again they seemed to be speaking silently among themselves, their faces reacting to unheard words. He waited, his mouth dry. Hoping the plan would work.

"How will they not be able to find your ship?"

"Once I have landed, I will destroy all the tracking equipment. I will destroy the ship in such a way that it will report back to the supply ship that I have crashed and am dead."

"That will work?"

"They will think I'm dead, yes. And that the ship isn't salvageable. Whether or not they'll send someone down to look for me, I can't say."

"What is to stop them from sending more ships, to come back and look for scillion? Or to come and exterminate all of us."

"For weeks now, I have been reporting dwindling amounts of scillion that we are able to mine. In some cases, I haven't had to lie. One of the Lt. Generals has been hoarding it, for what purpose I'm not sure. I have just ordered an attack on his camp. He is the one who tried to kill me and my men in a brazen attack. The other camps have had other problems. Only one camp has been sending out scillion of any amount. That's about to stop. I will make it appear that this planet is nothing but a problem as far as mining is concerned. Not worth the effort."

"It is the way of the divine."

"I don't understand what that even means."

"The divine is a chemical that exists everywhere on this planet. It gets into your blood and changes the way your brain works. Your men are not as effective as they once were, am I right?"

"Most of these men are new to me. Some of them have good records, but not, they don't seem to live up to their past accomplishments."

"It is the divine, working on them. It hits those hardest who resist the most."

"It has affected me, hasn't it?"

"It affects everyone. Why do you think you'd be an exception?" she asked.

Kalju started to answer, but has no idea what to say. Why should he have been an exception? Kalju just assumed that because of his strong discipline and routine that he would be immune to such a distraction. That he would be able to carry on and do the work. That he was a powerful enough man to overcome any chemical that didn't kill him.

At that moment, there was a knock on the door.

"Enter," Kal`ju said.

Two security guards brought in the Gonsha. Its hands secured behind the back.

The Gonsha ran to the others, who swarmed around it, making crooning noises.

"Remove the cuffs," Kalju said.

One of the men moved forward, all the Gonsha snarled at him, displaying three rows of teeth on the top. Perhaps even on the bottom of their mouths, too. Kalju couldn't see.

"He wants to remove the handcuffs," the woman said, gesturing with her hands.

One of the Oachnik said something to the Gonsha and they allowed the soldier to remove the restraints. The soldier moved quickly away from them after he finished.

"Dismissed," Kalju said.

The two guards hurried out the door, which slid closed behind them. The Gonsha stared at Kalju as if they'd like to eat him alive.

"I've done as you asked. The Lt. General who took it, him, prisoner has been reprimanded. He is the most incompetent man I've ever worked with."

They spoke silently among themselves for a third time.

The woman said, "You will need to release the villagers and Council Member who you hold prisoner."

"I was going to do that anyway," Kalju said. "You may take them with you when you leave today. Although I'm not sure if they wouldn't be safer in this butte, than down in the village. I have launched an attack on one of the Lt. Generals. If he's survived, and if he can, he will retaliate."

"We will help you rid this planet of the rest of the Caledonians. We cannot risk further poisoning of our water. This is a small planet," she said.

"We will need to coordinate the timing," he said.

For the plan to succeed, timing was crucial.

The woman turned back to the Oachnik and asked, "Who will communicate with the others?"

A tall, gangly looking Oachnik said, "I will."

"You will need to coordinate with the Governor General here."

The Oachnik came over and asked to see the map again. The woman was speaking to the Gonsha.

Then one of them came over and said, "I will communicate with my people. We are great warriors and will help in the battle."

The two of them spoke and planned, Kalju chimed in with timing suggestions.

A message pinged in. The attack on Lassorn was over. They'd thrown everything they could at him. The mining camp and Naritana were now holes in the ground. No telling if Lassorn was dead or alive. Most of the flyers were on their way back to base. Two had landed on nearby buttes. The men were spying on the camp. Waiting to see if anyone came out.

Kalju watched the woman talk to the others, putting plans into motion. Would he be able to pull an escape off?

Did he really want to go underground with these people? It might take years before he could get off the planet on a supply ship.

Could he live here with the divine?

No ready answer came.

CHAPTER 27 - CASSANDRA

It took much more time to leave New Kasbah than it did to get there. Along with the Gonsha prisoner, they brought all the Council Members, any of their family who had remained on Titania, and the imprisoned villagers. Altogether forty-three people. Most of whom didn't have food with them and some who couldn't move very quickly, so it was slow going.

Cassandra didn't care. She was pleased to be able to get all her people away from the Caledonians. Whether they'd make it to safety remained to be seen. They decided to stop at the Gonsha village on the way to the Oachnik sanctuary. It was closer to the Council Complex. Cassandra wasn't sure that was a good idea, but Xixia demanded it.

Age-old enemies. Completely outnumbered. What could possibly go wrong?

The Gonsha lived in a cavern deeper than the Oachnik ever went, Xixia told her. The Oachnik believed the deep depths of the planet were sacred and not for the living. Only spirits lived there.

The air felt warm, damp and humid. Water dripped from the walls and a sort of strange algae grew on the cave walls. Maybe it was moss. There was fungi growing everywhere. Some of it glowed in the darkness, casting eerie shadows. The smell was musty and moldy. Even the lobby of the Council Complex hadn't been this humid.

They stopped in a massive underground cave with a stream running through it. Which was where many of the Gonsha lived but not all, Annou, the mother of the imprisoned young one told her. There were other villages of large numbers. They would all agree to help rid the planet of the intruders.

There were hundreds, perhaps thousands of Gonsha. Bluish, silver fur as far as she could see, until it blended into the darkness lurking at the edges of the light. If the Gonsha wanted to do them harm, there would be no stopping them.

The mother of the imprisoned Gonsha stood on a tall, carved boulder and spoke in their guttural language. Cassandra could pick out a word or two. It was a similar language to Oachnik, maybe even created from the same roots.

The other parent, Pannatta, Cassandra couldn't tell if it was male or female, interpreted for them in the common language.

"This is very important, please listen. What happened today will change our world. We were in the upper caverns when we were attacked by the strangers with black fur. We killed many, but they overwhelmed us with their guns. Many of us were killed too." She listed seven names. "They took Orrou. We couldn't follow. They had too many people with guns. We followed as far as we could."

Annou pointed at them. "This human with the removable green fur, and these Oachnik were traveling to the large butte to meet with the black-furred ones. To negotiate their leaving our home. They said they would try to get Orrou back. We said we would come too. This human, her name is Cassandra, spoke to the leader of the black-furred ones. He will make his people go away if we let him stay and hide him from his people. We agreed to help him make his people go away if he released all our people who had as prisoners. He has done so."

Annou turned slowly in a circle, addressing everyone in the cavern, using her hands to accentuate her words.

"We will attack their mining camps in just a few days. Chase them to their flyers and let some of them escape. The rest we will kill, until there is only their leader left on our world. The Oachnik and some humans will do the same. We will let their leader stay, he is touched by the divine, even though he resists her power. If he survives the transition, he will be a powerful friend. Then we will be at peace with the Oachnik again, as we were in the ancient past, before the rift. We will all take apart the mining camps that poison our water. The humans will help us clean the mining camps. Then our lives will be even better than before. Long have we waited to take our place again in this world. We have paid dearly for our ancestors' guilt. It is time for us to go to the surface again."

The crowd thundered and roared so loud, Cassandra covered her ears. The ground shook from the stomping of their feet. The Oachnik around her widened their eyes until gold showed around the edges. She had never seen them so afraid.

"One of the mining camps has been destroyed already. Some of you will be sent to make sure no black-furred ones have escaped. The rest of you will ready yourselves for battle or for caring for those fighting. Pannatta will tell you where to travel. The other villages will join us. Once everything is complete, we will all gather at the large butte. On the surface. To claim our place in this world again. So go now. We must feed our guests and let them rest. They must travel for several days, to safety and to speak with their people."

The crowd roared again, not so long this time. Pannatta left us as he went to organize the attacks.

A smaller hunched-over Gonsha motioned to them and led us to a group of smooth, carved stones. They were all flat and the same size. Perfect for sitting on. Cassandra gratefully sat down.

Stone bowls with some sort of meat in a broth were brought out. Metal spoons were handed out and Cassandra ate, just now realizing how hungry she'd been.

The meat had a mild flavor, the sauce was spicy and almost hot. Like chili peppers. Her nose cleared and she could smell, just then realizing she'd been plugged up. There were bits of plants floating around in the broth, but she couldn't identify them. The meal filled her up and left her feeling sated.

Soft pads were brought out for everyone. When was the last time she'd slept? A couple days ago at least. Cassandra spread her sleepsack on one, and fell asleep as soon as she lay horizontal.

When Cassandra woke, the huge cavern was nearly empty of Gonsha. She sat up in her sleepsack. The Oachnik were awake, gathered near a fire and eating again. The humans were still sleeping. They'd been kept prisoner and inactive so long that the trek here had worn them all out.

She got up, rolled up her sleepsack and stuffed it into her pack. Then went over to the fire. One of the Oachnik youngsters ladled up a bowl full of the same stew they'd had before they slept.

"What kind of meat is it?" she asked.

"Sikkin," said the Oachnik. "They live deep in the caves. We don't usually go deep enough to hunt them."

Cassandra sat down on one of the smooth rocks by the fire. "Will your people work with the Gonsha?" she asked Xixia.

"We will do as the elders ask. They have long suspected the Gonsha still lived. And have wanted peace between us. The Gonsha have paid for what their ancestors did. Let us hope they are all as desirous for peace as those who were here last night seem to be."

"I hope so too. Peace is good. There is no reason why all of us can't live together and get on with our lives." Cassandra hoped that was true. "What will we do with the Caledonian?"

Xixia shrugged. "He will have much work to do. To understand all that the divine has given him. He will either overcome his fears or he will succumb to madness. There is nothing we can do. That is his battle to fight."

"I hope he wins it. Or if he loses, then he goes quietly and alone. I'd hate for him to take any of us with him," said Cassandra.

"He has already taken a great many Caledonians with him," said Xixia.

After eating, they woke the all the villagers and packed up, readying themselves for a long trek deeper into the cave system. To safety.

CHAPTER 28 - KALJU

Kalju waited an appropriate amount of time, then changed the alert status. Orange alert. Everything locked down. All soldiers in place, ready to repel an attack. He sent word to the mining camps that attacks were expected.

He'd sent all his security off to sleep. To rest, just in case the imminent attacks should happen.

"I want you at your sharpest then. I don't need you now."

Then he continued with his plans. He removed all but one tracking device from his personal flyer. Packed a bag of essentials. Clothes that he'd stolen from the village. Civilian clothes. He put his bag of clothes, food and water into the flyer.

When everything was ready, he sent a signal to the Oachnik.

He timed out the hour the Oachnik had said they needed to get everyone in place.

Then he got in his flyer, took off and sent out the message to all the Caledonians.

"Under attack! We are under attack! Everyone to their flyers and up to the ship orbiting above. Evacuation! Get every man off the planet. Forget about equipment and supplies. Bring only weapons if possible and scillion if it's already loaded. Evacuate now!"

He set the message to repeat at least twice.

Then he flew high above, waiting and watching. He pinged his security team and told them he was already on a flyer headed for the ship in orbit.

At the Council Complex, flyers loaded up and left. There was more than enough space for everyone.

He switched off his radio and flew over the mining camps. By the time he got to Yutif's camp, it was empty. Crowds of Gonsha and Oachnik were celebrating. There was a small pile of bodies in black uniforms. Burning. Mining machinery was already in action, moving debris away from the river.

At Matton's, Camp #3, the mining machinery was in action, moving the mountain of debris to cover the camp's buildings. He didn't see any bodies.

At Lassorn's camp, Naritana, everything was black and burned out, from the attack Kalju had launched. The Oachnik and Gonsha were burning a few bodies there as well.

Flying over Ritgan's camp, Santia, was much the same. A few burning bodies and mining debris being moved. The small city nearby looked untouched. A group of civilians standing by, were being guarded by Oachnik. They would probably be unharmed.

The evacuation had gone off smoothly. He hoped Caledonia stayed off the planet.

He turned the radio back on and said, "Evacuation complete. I'll be coming shortly. Prepare to leave orbit."

He headed the flyer off over the desert, on autopilot. He removed his wristband and changed into the civilian clothes. He slid the pack on and then a chute.

The radio crackled, "Governor General Kepa, your trajectory isn't moving towards us."

"I have one more thing I need to check out," he said. "Then I'm coming. Prepare to leave orbit as instructed."

Kalju unsheathed a knife and cut into the flap of skin between his left thumb and forefinger to remove the bead-sized, personal tracking device. It hurt like hell, but at least the tracker wasn't in too deep.

Blood streamed and he sprayed sealant on the wound and slapped a bandage on it. That would have to be enough for now.

He dove the flyer towards a rocky mountain, waiting until the last possible minute before blasting the flyer's door off.

"Damned equipment. Flyer door just flew off." Then he yelled, "Under attack. Leave orbit immediately. Without me."

Kalju jumped, pulled the parachute open. Pushed his body so he'd move away from the flyer.

The flyer continued to dive. Streaming towards the rocky mountain. Hitting and exploding into many pieces.

Kalju felt the heat. One of the flyer's pieces shot through his chute. Catching it on fire. He fell fast. Too fast. Aimed towards a sandy spot.

Landed too hard. Felt both his legs crunch and give out. Then he passed out. Still falling.

When he woke, Kalju felt a gentle rocking sensation. He must be at home. On Caledonia, on the water, sleeping in a boat.

Except he heard strange voices and opened his eyes. It was almost completely dark. He could see rock above him. He was lying flat on his back and moving through a tunnel. Underground. The voices were Oachnik.

"Where am I?" he asked.

"You are safe," said one of them in the common language.

What the hell did that mean? Why was he here?

Then he remembered everything. He couldn't feel his legs at all. His hand hurt. Where the tracker no longer was.

Was he really safe? Had he pulled it off? Gotten free of Caledonia?

Only time would answer that. But his legs? He knew they were broken. Perhaps the Oachnik had fixed them and given him painkillers.

At least he was free of Lassorn. And hopefully all the others. The cruiser should leave. He'd ordered them to. One of the Lt.

Generals would be in charge by now. Command would have appointed one of the survivors by now. Depending on who that was, Command might have negated his order.

Might.

That had always been a possibility.

The next time Kalju woke, he was in a massive cavern. Fire glowed against the darkness. He caught a whiff of the smoke. A human hovered over him. A big man who Kalju recognized as one who'd been imprisoned at the Council Complex. The one with mechanical legs.

"How are you feeling?" asked the man. "I'm Thomas, the Doctor."

"I don't know. Alive, I guess."

"That's a good thing," said Thomas.

"Can be. How much damage did I do to my legs?"

The man looked grim.

"What does that mean?" asked Kalju.

"They're gone. We couldn't reattach them. Not me, not the Oachnik or Gonsha healers."

"What do you mean gone?"

"From mid-thigh down. The knees were shattered and mostly severed by rock. Not anything I'd wish on my worst enemy, considering I'm the same way."

Kalju lay there. He could feel his legs, couldn't he? He felt like he was wiggling his toes.

"I don't believe you," he said.

"I'll help you sit up," said Thomas.

He helped Kalju sit up. A wave of dizziness and nausea passed through him. Then when he nodded, the Doctor moved to the side of him and pulled the fur covering back.

Kalju was naked from the waist down and his legs bare. They were cut off at mid-thigh, just like Thomas said. The stumps wrapped in sterile, white bandage.

Kalju looked at them in horror. He'd planned to live out the rest of his life a free man. Free to travel where he wanted. To walk other planets. To work his way to the far end of the galaxy, away from Caledonia's reach.

That was no longer possible. He didn't have the credits to afford good tech. He'd be stuck with cheap mechanical legs like this Doctor. Which would limit where he could go and what he could do.

He lay back down and Thomas covered him again with the animal hide.

"Want to talk?" asked Thomas.

Kalju shook his head and closed his eyes.

"I'll have some food sent over. You need to eat."

Kalju said nothing. He was a cripple. He'd never really walk again. This damned planet had done this to him. The divine had done this. He hated everything about this place.

He sipped a cup of the soup one of the Oachnik brought him. He didn't speak and neither did the Oachnik.

He had nothing to say. No reason to think his life was worth living any more. Why hadn't he just stayed in the flyer when it crashed? It would have been better. He'd never have a reason to be alive now.

Had he ever?

CHAPTER 29 - CASSANDRA

CASSANDRA SAT ON A BOULDER DEEP IN THE CAVES FEELING THE explosions above. She didn't know if it was the native warriors or the Caledonians fighting back. It didn't really matter. Dirt and occasionally chunks of rock came from the ceiling above.

She took a deep breath, trying to release the fear that the whole cave would come tumbling down around her. That she'd die alone, surrounded by rubble, all entryways blocked, unable to find a way out.

Cassandra shook her head and took another deep breath. Xixia left the group of Oachnik she'd been with and came over to Cassandra sitting down on her haunches next to her. She took her hand and set it on Cassandra's, patting it.

"It will be all right, dear."

"Will it?" asked Cassandra.

"Of course. Or else it won't and we'll all die."

"Aren't you ever afraid of the whole thing caving in?"

"Those sorts of things rarely happen in this area. We are in one of the safe caves. Then again, that's why the Council banned all explosives, except those used by qualified geologists. The miners aren't allowed to blow things up randomly."

"But then the Caledonians came."

"Yes. We will have to inspect all the cave systems after all this. And abandon or shore up those that are dangerous. The Gonsha have been doing that for years. I hadn't realized."

"You didn't know they existed," said Cassandra.

"No, we didn't."

The explosions had stopped.

Xixia listened and said, "Raspin is above us. On the surface. He says all the ships have left the Council Complex. They will go check to see if it's abandoned, like the Caledonian said it would be."

"I hope it is. I hope they've left the planet."

She sipped some of the stale water from her bottle. It was warm, too. Living in New Kasbah had spoiled her.

The Oachnik gathered together and prayed. As did the few Gonsha with them. Only the humans had no gods left. They'd mostly left them behind when they took to the enormous void of space. Keeping only reverence and wonder at the vastness of the universe. Gone was the solid belief in an earthbound god or goddess. Or even in a sky deity.

Still, humans huddled together in a community built out of respect, need and compassion. Which is more than had happened on old Earth, according to what little history she knew of the place.

It seemed to take forever for Raspin to report back. They had been attacked by one frightened soldier up on the surface. They'd killed the man, who hadn't seemed quite sane. No other Caledonians had been found. He confirmed that the Council Complex was completely deserted. No Caledonians, no prisoners. No Oachnik or Gonsha.

There was a cheer from those in the cavern.

They began the trek upwards. With all the villagers, and the elderly Gonsha who'd come with them to safety, it was slow going. Although Cassandra was hard put to keep up with the elderly Gonsha. They were hardy folk.

When they reached the surface, the sun was rising. A beautiful, fiery sunrise streaking the sky red, salmon and bright orange. She smelled the fresh, dry air and felt at home again.

It was a half a day's walk to New Kasbah and the Council Complex.

By the time they'd reached the village, they'd been joined by many other groups of Oachnik and Gonsha.

Xixia kept giving her reports. "Sualla sends word that the Caledonians have left Santia. Except for a few who were killed. Xaxian has been hiding in the caves since Naritana was attacked by Caledonians, last week. Luckily, she'd been gathering herbs in the mountains nearby during the attack or she would have been killed. A few Caledonians survived that attack and were hiding in nearby caves. They are now dead."

"How many mining camps did the Caledonians have?" asked Cassandra.

"Four. Plus their men at the Council Complex. I have heard from three of the camps so far. Just one left."

They walked on, through the growing heat, which felt good. Cassandra took off her light coat and rolled up her sleeves, enjoying the feel of the sun on her skin.

New Kasbah stood empty and very dusty. No one had cleaned their windows or watered their plants. Dead, dried out plants littered pots and entryways. It looked like a ghost town.

Looking at her abandoned village made her sad. She longed to go off down the side street to her home and shop, tidy up. Sweep the floors, resume her life, but there would be time for that later. She stayed with the others.

By the time they made it to the Council Complex, they'd heard from all the mining camps. The Caledonians were gone. Off the planet or dead. Except for the Governor General. Perhaps he was gone or dead too. She hadn't heard.

At the Council Complex hordes of Oachnik and Gonsha gathered. There were only a handful of humans in comparison. Marita and those Cassandra had originally left New Kasbah with had returned. Along with the villagers who'd been taken prisoner.

Cassandra hugged Marita who grinned at her and said, "I have some news for you."

"Oh?"

"Good news. I'm moving in with Samuel when we return to New Kasbah."

"Congratulations," said Cassandra. She hadn't even noticed a romance blooming between the two, so distracted by everything else. It seemed an unlikely match, but they were both kind, gentle people and she wished them well.

Colin, Aggripina and Mazin stood talking to each other. Finally, Colin went towards the speaking stone, but not before passing a very pale Alexander and embracing him again.

As Colin climbed up on the stone, the crowd hushed, waiting for him.

"I am Colin Schuante, a former Council Member. Today, Titania has accomplished a great thing. With the coming together of Oachnik, Gonsha, a few humans, and a fair amount of luck, we have rid ourselves of the Caledonians. I do not know if they will return, but with our unity, we shall prevail."

The crowd roared at this.

He continued, "Too long has Titania been ruled by humans with a small representation of Oachnik. The Gonsha have been completely unheard. This cannot continue. As of today we must be ruled by the elders of all beings on this planet. We truly need all our wisdom to move forward. I do not know how we will accomplish this, but it will happen."

The crowd yelled and stamped again.

Cassandra looked around. She was on a slight rise and could see the masses of Gonsha and Oachnik well, even though they were taller than her by a couple of feet. There must have been at least seven hundred beings. Maybe more.

She hadn't known that many natives even existed on the planet. And there must be several other gatherings like this happening at the other camps. Although perhaps most of the Oachnik and Gonsha were here. She spotted the group of elder

Oachnik and at least two of the elder Gonsha. She had a feeling most of the Gonsha had lived in caves other than the one she'd visited.

She caught the end of Colin's speech. "We have an exciting future ahead of us, now that everyone will be involved. I can hardly wait to see how we work together and to learn from my new colleagues."

He bowed to the elders as he stepped down and gestured for them to speak.

The silver-furred Oachnki stood upon the speaking stone.

"I am Assalia, of the Cantania Clan. We are warriors. Long have we determined who lived on this world. We allowed those humans who were willing to partner with us in caring for our home. Those who are present here, and their ancestors. We restricted mining to those places which were stable. The Caledonians overwhelmed us. We did not expect them to be so powerful, or to cause the damage that they have so quickly. We foolishly believed they would care for our home as other humans have done. We need help caring for our world, from the Gonsha and the humans. We must never allow such a thing to happen again. We underestimated our enemy. This is a great failing in a warrior. We are shamed to have allowed those onto our land, those who have poisoned our water."

Cassandra was shocked at the elder's feelings of shame. How could they possibly have prevented the Caledonians from landing? The humans hadn't had enough power to stop them either.

Assalia continued, "We will need to work more closely with the humans and the Gonsha. The universe is such a vast space and we have only lived on our own world. We must work to prevent anything like this from happening ever again."

She bowed, stepped down and nodded to the Gonsha elders.

Annou moved forward to speak.

"I am Annou, of the Long-Claw Clan. We Gonsha have hidden for many generations. Long have we paid for the crime of our ancestors. Our ancestors who thought they could rule this world alone. Without the Oachnik. They tried to kill every Oachnik. After we were banished to the depths of this planet, we had long, long dark times to think. To consider what we should have done. The divine spoke to us. She kept us in her heart. We have grown in number as a people. We have grown in intelligence. And we have grown our hearts larger. We wish for peace, but we will also fight fiercely for this planet. We wish to live our lives on the surface again, to see the sun, even though the darkness brings many gifts. We wish to take our place among this new alliance, with humans and Oachnik. We do not claim to understand your ways. We have much to learn about who you are and where we can best fit into this world. We are eager to learn and to live once again with others."

She bowed and stepped off the speaking stone.

Colin returned to it and said, "Thank you Assalia and Annou, for speaking for your people. We elders will meet again tomorrow morning when the sun comes up. On the top floor of the Council Chamber. Today, we celebrate, but we will keep a wary eye out for the Caledonians. They might decide to return. Their ship is still orbiting above."

Cassandra whispered, "Go away. And don't ever return, there is nothing here for you."

CHAPTER 30 - KALJU

Kalju sat just outside the mouth of the cave, looking down at the small fields below. The Gonsha had irrigated them with channels of water from the nearby river and the water flowed where they unblocked the channels.

He stripped open another pod and pulled out the small soft seeds with his fingers, putting them into the clay bowl in his lap. Which was about all he could do.

In Caledonia it would have been called women's work. That was about all he was suited for these days, but found he didn't mind it. It was relaxing meditative work. Much better than worrying about whether someone was trying to kill you or not.

Since he'd woken up missing both his legs from mid-thigh down, Thomas, the doctor, had made him a pair of mechanical legs. Kalju was trying to strengthen his muscles and get the balance right. He still used a crutch on one side. When he improved, he'd graduate to a cane. Perhaps. He didn't mind so much. He had nowhere to go. Nothing to do, but he was alive and free.

For the first time in his entire life.

Caledonia hadn't returned to search for his body, which

relieved him. The ship had waited a few days, then left orbit. He hoped they'd given up Titania as a lost cause.

He'd stayed with the humans for a couple of weeks, until his stumps and hand were healed. Then when the mechanical legs were ready, one of the date growers had given him a ride on his mechanical produce cart. To where the Gonsha were beginning to farm again. With decades-old seeds. They'd been sealed in clay pots for a time when the Gonsha returned to the surface of the planet.

He'd watched them prepare the soil, spreading it with moss gathered from the cave depths. Letting the moss rot and turning the soil over. Then digging irrigation channels and planting the seeds. It only took days till the entire field was covered with green velvet. It was as if they'd never stopped being farmers. Their knowledge certainly hadn't been lost.

And now, a month later, he was cleaning the mouta, little green seeds. They would be cooked in a broth until soft, Pannatta told him.

Kalju picked up another pod and emptied it, tossing the empty pod into a mesh basket. The pods, he'd been told, would be returned to the fields and dug in, fertilizing a crop of a vegetable the Gonsha had yet to plant.

When he was stronger, Kalju decided, he would spend some time with the Oachnik. To see how they lived. Sit at night and listen to their stories.

He'd learned so much from the Gonsha. Their world view was so alien to his own. It made him reassess everything he'd ever learned. It was either that or go insane.

Women, for instance.

On Caledonia, women were pampered things. They were scarce. Valuable property, going from their father's house, bought and paid for by their husband. Most men couldn't afford a wife. He could have, but it would have been a waste. Command had always been sending him off on some far away assignment.

Here, female Gonsha, Oachnik and even humans, were

warriors. Fighting alongside the men. With the Gonsha, the women did as much work, and the same kind, as the men. Digging the water channels, turning over the soil. Some of them stayed with the children, as did some of the men. It puzzled him at first. He'd always thought of children as being the provenance of women. Clearly, things were different here. Very different.

He decided that the second half of his life would be spent rearranging his mind. Rethinking the order of things. He'd always thought the way Caledonia did things was the only right way. He was unsure if this new desire to explore the universe was the result of the divine working on him, or if it was the result of losing his legs and his ability to physically move forward into life.

He was broken.

And yet, perhaps he was healing in ways that even he couldn't have foreseen. At some point, he'd return to New Kasbah and live with the villagers. To see what they were like. He'd wait for a year or more though, until he was sure Caledonia wouldn't return. And in the meantime, he'd explore the world of the Gonsha and the Oachnik. Trying to really understand who they were. And see if their worldview didn't make him feel more at home. Because this really was his home now. There was no other.

CHAPTER 31 - CASSANDRA

CASSANDRA WOKE JUST AS THE SUN HIT HER WINDOW, ILLUMINATING and warming the entire room. The smell of amber lingered in the air. She'd burned some incense yesterday in the shop and the scent had traveled up to her bedroom. She stretched, trying to decide whether to get up or lie in bed longer.

Up, she decided.

Once up, Cassandra changed into silky long pants the orange of the flaming sunrise. She put on a loose turquoise top with it, plus tan sandals. And a moonstone pendant. Then brushed her long gray hair and plaited it into a braid.

After a breakfast of toasted flatbread, spread with soft goat cheese and chopped dates, she took her cup of wassia berry tea down to the shop. She propped open the door, turned on the lights and gazed around. She felt so grateful to be home again. And yet, everything was different now.

Oachnik and Gonsha came into her shop. To marvel at the pretty things. And to get readings and consultations. Humans, of course, still came. More of them than she'd ever met before.

Everyone was making more of an effort towards unity and in the process they were reinventing themselves and their world.

Marita and Samuel were expecting a baby. Colin had become

head of the Council. The Council who quickly barred the former Council Members re-admittance to Titania 37, those who'd tucked tail and ran when the Caledonians came.

The Council had decided against applying to the Coalition of Planets, deciding it would bring more problems than it solved. Besides, many Coalition Planets were now under Caledonian control, so it didn't seem to be very effective.

Instead, they began sending out reports about the divine and how it altered people. That, combined with the first-hand accounts of Caledonian soldiers kept most people away. And left them all alone to govern themselves as they wanted.

Which made Cassandra quite happy. She had just enough business to keep her solvent and lots of new friends.

And she'd learned that people's futures weren't set in stone. That even the fate of an entire planet could be changed, with care and cooperation. Even a Caledonian could change, or so she'd heard. Some day she'd look him up and find out if he really had changed.

Living with the Oachnik had certainly changed her. Cassandra's reverence for life had vastly increased.

As it should.

IF YOU'VE GOTTEN this far, would you please consider leaving an honest review? Many readers depend on reviews to help them find their next read. It doesn't take much, just a few words on your opinion of the book. It would mean so much to me. Thank you!

Author of *To the Stars and Back Again*
LINDA JORDAN
TITANIAN
FURY
Bloody Revenge, the Best Refuge

ABOUT THE AUTHOR

Linda Jordan writes fascinating characters, visionary worlds, and imaginative fiction. She creates both long and short fiction, serious and silly. She believes in the power of healing and transformation, and many of her stories follow those themes.

In a previous lifetime, Linda coordinated the Clarion West Writers' Workshop as well as the Reading Series. She spent four years as Chair of the Board of Directors during Clarion West's formative period. She's also worked as a travel agent, a baker, and a pond plant/fish sales person, you know, the sort of things one does as a writer.

Currently, she's the Programming Director for the Writers Cooperative of the Pacific Northwest.

Linda now lives in the rainy wilds of Washington state with her husband, daughter, four cats, a cluster of Koi and an infinite number of slugs and snails.

Her other work includes:

Falling Into Flight
Paradiso Stories
To the Stars and Back Again
Aboard the Universe

All her work can be found at your favorite online bookseller.

Get a FREE ebook!

Sign up for Linda's Serendipitous Newsletter at her website: www.LindaJordan.net

Visit her at: www.LindaJordan.net
She can be found on Facebook at:
www.facebook.com/LindaJordanWriter
Metamorphosis Press website is at:
www.MetamorphosisPress.com
Goodreads: https://www.goodreads.com/author/show/2021274.Linda_Jordan

Writers love reviews, even short, simple ones and honest reviews help other readers find the book. Please go to where you bought this book, or Goodreads, and leave a review. It would be much appreciated.